HOW TO SAVE A
SUPERHERO

HOW TO SAVE A
SUPERHERO

RUTH FREEMAN

HOLIDAY HOUSE · NEW YORK

HOLIDAY HOUSE is registered in the U.S. Patent and Trademark Office.

Printed and bound in August 2021 at Maple Press, York, PA, USA.

www.holidayhouse.com

First Edition

1 3 5 7 9 10 8 6 4 2

Library of Congress Cataloging-in-Publication Data

Names: Freeman, Ruth, 1951– author.

Title: How to save a superhero / Ruth Freeman.

Description: First edition. | New York : Holiday House, [2021] | Audience:
Ages 8–12. | Audience: Grades 4–6. | Summary: Fifth-grader Addie and
two other children who spend afternoons at the Happy Valley retirement
community, where their mothers work, investigate whether one of the
residents is a superhero.

Identifiers: LCCN 2020050863 (print) | LCCN 2020050864 (ebook) | ISBN
9780823447626 (hardcover) | ISBN 9780823450220 (ebook)

Subjects: CYAC: Retirement communities—Fiction. | Old age—Fiction.
Ability—Fiction. | Superheroes—Fiction.

Classification: LCC PZ7.1.F7547 How 2021 (print) | LCC PZ7.1.F7547
(ebook) | DDC [Fic]—dc23

LC record available at https://lccn.loc.gov/2020050863

LC ebook record available at https://lccn.loc.gov/2020050864

ISBN: 978-0-8234-4762-6 (hardcover)

To my uncle Mickey Macfarlan,
the inspiration for an aging superhero,
and to little Ned and Mac,
superheroes-to-be

CHAPTER 1

The map was no help at all. Fat raindrops fell from the trees overhead, hit the ink drawing, and turned the lines into blurry blue rivers and splotches. Wet leaves blew down and stuck to her raincoat like postage stamps. Everything around her smelled lost and lonely.

Was this really the right way? Uncle Tim and his brother-in-law, Matt, had said to follow the stream. Was that what they called this ditch going down between the trees with a trickle of dirty water in it? Addie wished her mom had shown her the way instead of giving her a pat, and a bit of a push, on the back and a "You're good at maps, Addie. You'll figure it out. You always do. And I'll see you when you get there."

A squeaky voice behind her made her jump.

"I've seen the most unusual insects in September."

It was this little kid with a huge backpack coming up behind her. Because he never took his eyes off the ground, he had to push his glasses up his nose about every other second.

He talked in a slow, precise kind of way like he was some scientist in a lab coat.

"Once...I found a caterpillar...with white bristles...and red spikes on its tail...like horns." And he walked extra slow too, prying up stones and rotten sticks with one toe. When he squatted down to get a closer look at something, his backpack made him look like one of those million-year-old tortoises.

"Want to see a slug?" Not getting an answer, he looked up, his excitement fading. "Is that a map? Are you lost or something?"

"No, I'm good," said Addie, turning and walking away into the woods.

"Okay. Well, see ya." He launched his backpack into place and began to wander off.

Addie stopped. Face-to-face with one tree after another, she had to admit she had no idea where she was going.

"Wait!" she called before the kid got too far away. "Do you know where Happy Valley Village is?"

"Sure," he said over his shoulder. "That's where I'm going."

And that was how Addie found her way: by following this kid called Dickson down the rocky path he called the ravine to the retirement place where his mother and Addie's mother both worked. She also found out, though she certainly hadn't asked, that he was in fourth grade, a year behind Addie, he had skipped first grade because he was so smart, and slugs have green blood.

Following him was slow going, since he kept stopping to poke around in the dirt. At least Addie didn't have to talk to him. While Bug Boy droned on with some new bit of information, Addie looked at the trees that arched over her, shutting out most of the afternoon light. It wasn't like Mount Repose, Maine, where she and her mom, Tish, had lived with Granny Lu. That was spruce country, where zillions of needles combed the wind soft as a sigh and the air smelled of Christmas trees. Here, in Pennsylvania, there were leaves. Leaves rustling like colored paper, falling thick like pencil shavings and sticking to the soggy ground, where they settled into the mud and smelled of mold.

She and Tish had lived with Granny Lu ever since Addie was born. Addie's mom was the youngest after four brothers. Definitely the baby of the family, until she grew up and had Addie when she was seventeen.

Addie was short for Adelaide. The story was that Granny Lu had cornered Tish one day when she was pregnant.

Addie could just picture it: Granny Lu asking in her gravelly voice, which did a good job of hiding the tenderness inside:

"So, Tish, got any baby names in mind?"

⁎

Knowing Tish, she had probably shrugged and tried to ignore her mother. As the one and only girl in the family, Tish had been named after Granny Lu's own dear, sweet mother, Letitia, maybe because Granny Lu was hoping to pass some of that sweetness on to her baby girl.

Granny Lu went on to say that if Tish's baby girl was named after one of Granny Lu's dearly beloved sisters, Granny Lu would leave all her money to Tish and Addie.

Well, Tish always said Granny Lu had a sense of humor. Tish didn't think anything in Granny Lu's house was worth more than $3.50, but you never can be sure, can you? So Adelaide it was, and Addie she became. Which, in the long run, wasn't so bad, since the other sisters were Eunice and Leona, and, thank goodness, no one had suggested using Granny Lu's real name, which was Lucretia.

Life with Granny Lu had been pretty good, especially when she and Tish were getting along. Granny Lu had opened Lulu's House of Hair in her extra bedroom even before her husband died young. There was one chair for clients in front of a jeweled mirror, one chair at a sink, and one attached to a dome hair dryer. Twinkly lights went across the ceiling. A tinselly pink Christmas tree came out in November and stayed till February, when the strings of red hearts came out. Granny Lu was into seasonal decorations and bought way, way too many things on Home Shopping TV.

As soon as she was old enough, Addie was put in charge of decorations and sweeping up for an allowance. She loved leaving the school bus behind and running up the walk to chat with Mrs. Donald about the weather, or make Ms. Schmidt a mug of tea, or see the latest pictures of Mrs. Leroux's cat.

The one unbreakable rule was that no client was kept past 4 p.m., because that was when Granny Lu and Addie had business to attend to. Some days it was Home Shopping TV. "That commemorative coin is going to be worth a jackpot someday...just you wait and see!" And some days it was exercising with their favorite videos, such as *Bollywood Dance Craze*. Addie and Granny Lu had matching rainbow leggings. Granny Lu was all about keeping up with the latest styles in clothes, haircuts, and eye shadows, and she tried to pass this along to Addie, without much success. Addie didn't care much about looking good, but she definitely liked the dance routines, and the decorations for each season, and she loved Granny Lu.

Then Granny Lu died and everything changed.

Since then, Addie and Tish had bounced around to each of Tish's brothers, with a few cousins thrown in. They were on the last ones: Nice Uncle Tim and Crazy Aunt Tina. Aunt Tina had a brother, Matt, who worked in landscaping at the Happy Valley Village Retirement Community, which was how Tim got his sister, Tish, a job there. Owing to a few minor run-ins Tish had had with the law, it wasn't easy, but Tim and Matt convinced them to try her for a month. So they had one month to make it work.

Addie didn't have high hopes, as Granny Lu would have put it. Tish wasn't one to put down roots and stick around anywhere for too long. This new school was Addie's eleventh, if you counted preschool.

"Wait till Wilma sees this millipede!"

Dickson was holding something with a lot of legs.

Addie gave a snort.

"She's in for a real treat. Who's Wilma?"

"You'll see. She works at Happy Valley Village… HVV, for short. There it is."

Addie stopped. At the bottom of the ravine the trickle had grown into a full-fledged stream and flowed into a wide, round pond. It was surrounded by a lawn that stretched up a sloping hill to the biggest old house Addie had ever seen. There was a round tower sticking up at one end, and a long grassy terrace edged by a low stone wall. On both sides of the old house were modern buildings stretching out from it like giant arms.

What made Addie stare, though, was how, at that moment, the sun burst from under the dark gray clouds like a spotlight turning every window to a blinding melting gold. Maples beside the house blazed like rubies and topazes.

Addie could barely breathe. *Maybe it's a sign,* she thought. Maybe things could turn out all right here. She thought she could feel something good starting down in her toes….

She shook her head. Whoa, who was she kidding? Granny Lu always said, among other things, "Don't get your high-flyin' hopes flyin' too high."

CHAPTER 2

Push that door buzzer three times. That's how they know it's me."

Dickson had his hands full of millipede.

They were standing at what Dickson called the back door, a heavy metal door next to a loading dock and big trash containers. As they waited, he held the millipede up to the remote camera staring down at them.

"Look, Wilma!"

The door was yanked open by the biggest brown-skinned woman Addie had ever come face-to-face with. Actually, it wasn't Wilma's face, which towered over them, but Wilma's generous chest that Addie stood in front of.

"Hi, kids," said Wilma, out of breath. "Okay, listen up." She bent down so her face was suddenly inches away from them. She had a big, husky whisper. "We are deep in Crazy Time here. You won't believe the trouble. Hey," she said, looking at Addie, "you're the new girl. What's your name?"

"Addie."

"Okay, Addie, hi there. I'm Wilma, head nurse on this hall. We'll get better acquainted, but for now you've both got to hide." She wiped her shiny forehead.

Dickson started to say, "What...?"

But Wilma didn't miss a beat.

"Dickson, honey, ditch the worm. We got a new resident today, the dude I was telling you about, and he's gone and disappeared. Everybody's hunting for him. Security, nurses, companions, even Mrs. Sloat herself. If she sees you there'll be all kinds of questions. Take Addie here and head right downstairs. Got it?"

Addie had just enough time to see a long carpeted hallway that looked like a fancy hotel before Wilma whisked them through a door marked STAIRS.

"I'll come get you two as soon as I can," she said. "And don't worry, Addie, I'll tell your mom you're here. What a first day on the job she's having!" She shut the door firmly behind them.

Dickson led the way down the stairs to the floor below. This hallway was nothing like the one above. Weak fluorescent lights in the ceiling flickered and hummed. On one side the wall was bare cinder blocks with no windows; on the other there were floor-to-ceiling wire cages.

"Hey, what is this, a prison?"

"Nah," said Dickson. "It's where the residents store their stuff they don't need. See? Each one has a room number on it. This is the one we want. Mrs. Firillo lets me use hers while I wait for my mother after school."

He fished a hidden key out through the chicken wire and opened the padlock. He swung the wire door open and disappeared into the darkness. In the thin, flickering light, Addie couldn't see where he'd gone.

Then a lamp switched on.

"Okay, come on in," he called.

She stuck her head in the doorway. Dickson was scrunched up at one end of a comfy sofa. The light from a standing lamp helped him see what was in a plastic tub beside him.

"Do you want chips or cookies?" he said, looking up. "Des from the kitchen leaves snacks here for me. And there's bottles of juice too. The food here is great."

Addie settled at the other end of the big brown sofa. This place was definitely weird and creepy, but pepperoni-pizza-flavored chips could make anything a little better.

"How long do we have to stay here?" she said.

Dickson hunched over a book, stuffing fistfuls of chips in his mouth.

"Depends. Until our mothers are done work. I've even taken a nap in here once or twice if my mother had a late meeting. If it's quiet upstairs, Wilma gets me, and we watch TV up in the lounge. But today, with all this stuff going on, who knows?"

He looked up from his book.

"That reminds me," he said, pointing at her. "I'm not supposed to be here. If you meet my mother, you

CANNOT tell her I come over right after school and hang out here, okay? I'm supposed to go to an after-school program called Future Economists, Entrepreneurs, Business Owners, and Learners, FEEBOL for short, but I hate it. I hang out here instead."

"Fine with me." Addie shrugged. She couldn't care less about him.

Dickson went right back to his book. He was done talking. It must be a good book, but Addie noticed that the big, splashy pictures weren't insects.

Unscrewing the top of a juice bottle, Dickson caught her staring. He showed her the cover.

"WWE," he said.

Addie didn't know what that meant.

"World Wrestling Entertainment," he said. "Just my MOST FAVORITE thing in the whole world! Look at this!"

He held up his right arm and made a fist, squeezing until his face turned red.

"See that?" he said, holding his breath. "That's muscle!"

Addie looked at the skinny arm poking out of his oversized T-shirt, which read I'VE GOT THE POWER! in lightning-flash letters. It wasn't worth a comment.

"Haven't you ever watched WWE on TV?"

Addie shook her head. She had no interest in keeping the conversation going, but he was waiting for an answer.

"My grandma and me were more into Home Shopping and Fitness TV." Though, Addie thought to herself,

Granny Lu might have gotten a kick out of those bare-chested guys in crazy costumes and spandex.

The look he gave her showed Dickson thought the conversation had clearly run out of gas. He went back to reading.

Cooped up with Bug Boy, Addie had nothing to do but look around the storage compartment. She wondered if Mrs. Firillo might be into Home Shopping TV too. Every inch was taken up with stuff. Chairs piled with boxes were crammed next to a coatrack filled with clothes bags. A birdbath held up a large clock with no hands. On the floor were bags of dog food and potting soil beside stacks of flowerpots. A tangle of Christmas lights lay on top of a bureau with a dusty mirror hanging above it.

Addie fished her map notebook out of her backpack. That was what she did when she got bored...say, for instance, if she found herself spending time in an old lady's storage compartment with nothing to do. Dickson might have his WWE, but she had her maps.

She flipped through the pages. There were maps of her old bedroom, Granny Lu's living room, the hair salon, the garage where they'd open the big door on hot summer afternoons to drink ice tea and watch TV or exercise. There was a map she'd made of the campsite by the ocean where Tish had taken Addie for what she called "glamping...glamorous camping!" after she'd had a fight with Granny Lu. By then Granny Lu was pretty sick and thin, and when they came back a week later, she was in the hospital.

Addie had wanted to show Granny Lu the map of the campsite and put it into the Dream Box where she and Granny Lu kept their special things. Addie had made the campsite over-the-top beautiful, way more beautiful than it really was. Granny Lu would have loved it. But when they got back, the house was filled with family coming and going to the hospital, friends and neighbors bringing food. When Addie saw Granny Lu in the hospital, she was still and very sleepy. She patted Addie's hand and couldn't say more than a few words. Later, Addie asked different people in the house about the Dream Box, but no one had seen it.

When they left the house two years ago, after it was rented out, she'd made maps of the roads they took to each of Tish's brothers' places so that, one day, she could find her way back. Kind of like a trail of bread crumbs in one of those old fairy tales. Addie thought Granny Lu would like to know she was keeping her bearings, keeping her feet on the ground, and holding on to some sense of direction.

She turned to a blank page. What would she draw now? She didn't feel like drawing the storage compartment. Maybe a map of Uncle Tim and Aunt Tina's house. She could draw their living room and use it for a treasure hunt map for Bella, who was two and a half. Addie had never lived with little kids before and wasn't sure at first what it would be like, but she found it was kind of fun to come home at the end of the day and be in a two-and-a-half-year old's world. She got Bella to dance along to music, sometimes getting eight-month-old

Logan to join them in his wheely walker. Aunt Tina even said no one could keep them busy like Addie.

Addie didn't know how long they'd be there but, for the moment, it was home. She would need to draw a map of Happy Valley Village when she got to know it better too. If Tish kept her job, that is.

As Addie was thinking about the new map, she didn't realize she was staring at the dusty mirror on the far wall. One minute she was zoned out, the next minute everything changed with a snap. There was nothing different to see or hear, but she knew. Absolutely. There was someone in the storage compartment with them.

It was the mirror. She held her breath. Everything looked the same as it had a second ago, but in the dusty mirror above the bureau, she saw it. An eye, so dark it seemed to beam a ray of pure energy through time and space. Straight at her.

CHAPTER 3

In front of the bureau and mirror was an overstuffed armchair with its back to her. Seeing the eye reflected in the mirror made Addie notice the tuft of scraggly gray hair sticking up from the chair. Nothing moved, not a hair, not a blink.

Then the hall door opened with such a bang, both Addie and Dickson jumped.

"Dickson, you there?" a man's voice called.

Dickson bounced off the sofa, crunching over the chips he dropped.

"Yeah, right here!" He shoved his feet into his sneakers without bothering to tie the laces. Dickson filled Addie in. "Brad. He's in charge of the gym. He's helping me train."

Addie could hear Brad before she saw him, and when he got to the doorway, she could see why. Brad, young and fit in an HVV hoodie and sweat pants, wore an ID badge around his neck with an impressive array of keys. He held a cell phone and heavy-duty flashlight in one hand, a large walkie-talkie that crackled and zapped in the other.

"Hey, Dickson, have you seen anyone down here?" Brad saw Addie on the sofa. "Hi, you're...?"

"That's Addie," said Dickson. "Her mother started working here today."

"Oh, Tish, yeah, I just met her," said Brad. "Hey, have either of you seen anyone?"

Addie shook her head.

"Brad, can I help you look?" said Dickson.

"I don't know. We've got a real situation going on here. Maybe it'd be better if you stayed out of the way."

"Oh, come on, at least let me check things out with you down here."

Brad thought a second.

"Okay, just the storage units, then I've got to do a sweep of the rest of the lower level."

"Do you have an extra flashlight?"

Brad pulled a flashlight from his bulging hoodie pocket and handed it to Dickson.

"Addie, you want to come?" said Dickson.

Addie thought a second, thinking about that feeling of someone else being in the storage compartment, but shook her head. She must have imagined it. "You'll be back, though, right?"

"Yeah, don't worry," said Dickson. He hopped after Brad, trailing long shoelaces behind him.

Addie could hear Brad's deep voice and Dickson's

chirps as they went down the hall, taking time to peer into every storage area.

She opened a bag of cookies and wished she had some music she could turn on.

Then she heard it. She caught her breath. A sound deep and low like distant thunder that Addie felt shuddering inside her before she actually heard it. It came again, only this time it was bigger, like breakers from the open ocean pounding the shore.

"Excuse me...trying to clear my throat." A growl of a voice came from the armchair. A hand like a giant claw gripped the chair's arm, and a head covered with wild hair appeared around the side.

"Is the coast clear?"

Underneath two bristly eyebrows, the old guy's eyes were startling, they were so dark and penetrating. That was the only word Addie could think of. It was like they had their own force field looking right through her to the other side and back again.

"I said, are they gone? Can I make my escape?"

Addie had turned to stone, but now she made herself breathe.

"Are you escaping?" she said, her voice wobbly.

"Well, what do you think I'm doing? Sitting here for the fun of it?"

Addie was not about to let him get away with that.

"How do I know?" she snapped.

He looked at her with those eyes.

"Stop looking at me like that," she muttered.

He glared at her, then sat back in the chair. He sighed. "I thought you were helping me make my escape."

When he spoke again, his voice had lost some of its fierceness.

"Are those cookies you're eating?" he said.

"Chocolate chip," said Addie.

There was a pause. She thought he would ask for some, but he didn't.

"Want some? There's plenty."

"I would appreciate it. I haven't eaten anything since breakfast."

She unwound herself from the sofa and gathered up a selection of cookies, chips, and juice. She could hear Brad and Dickson far down the hall.

She walked slowly around to the front of the chair, not sure what to expect. And there he was. A grizzled old bear of a man in a wrinkly tweed jacket. It was a large chair, but he took up most of it. He wasn't fat at all. He looked big and powerful and, like a bear, unpredictable. He watched her with those eyes of his.

"Here," she said, holding up snacks to take his eyes off her. "Chocolate chip, sour cream and chive, pepperoni pizza, French onion, or hot tamale, and juice: apple-strawberry-cranberry or mango-peach-pineapple."

"For crying out loud," he rasped, "can't they keep things simple anymore? Why do they have to go around messing everything up? Plain old apple juice, lemonade, maybe grape juice. That's all anybody needs."

"Okay, so here, take the chocolate chip cookies and

the apple juice and pretend the strawberries and cranberries aren't there."

He grumbled but he took them. Then he had trouble tearing the plastic bag of cookies open and unscrewing the juice bottle. Addie had to help.

"So, why are you escaping?"

He finished the whole bottle of juice first.

"Because I don't want to be here." He said it as if it couldn't be more obvious.

"Then why are you here?"

He kept eating cookies as if he didn't want to answer. Finally, it came out.

"I fell."

"So?"

"All right, I fell several times. I couldn't get up. So they insisted I come here till I get steadier on my feet."

" 'They,' who's 'they'?"

"The Queen of the Underworld is what I call her. Mrs. Sloat, the director of this place. She decreed I have to be here, and I agreed to do it...for a month. But when I arrived today, I changed my mind. Your friend Brad can get me going again at my house."

Addie noticed two gold-topped canes propped on the chair next to him.

"So, then, you really shouldn't be escaping."

"How kind of you to point that out."

"Well, my mom started working here today, and she's helped people with that kind of stuff. She only has a month too. To see if they like her."

He huffed. "Well, good luck to her. But I wouldn't get your hopes up. Mrs. Sloat doesn't like anybody."

"I know, I know. My grandma used to say life is nothing but a cold, wet smack in the kisser, right?"

He looked at her as if he was about to ask a question, then decided against it. He finished the cookies.

"I might try some of those awful chips," he said.

Addie handed him a bag.

"Where were you going to go if you escaped?"

"My house is just over there." He leaned his head in one direction. "I live in the old farmhouse. This whole place belonged to my family, but I had to sell it and now it's…this…institution." He snorted. "Happy Valley Village! Ha! It's not happy, it's not in a valley, and it's certainly not my idea of a village!"

He sounded disgusted. "But I get to live here as long as…well, Mrs. Sloat is just waiting for me to die so she can get her hands on the whole place. So that's why I have to get better and move home again."

He shook his head and growled. "Living here is a misery. I miss having my own things, I miss the peace and quiet, and I miss my workshop. I'm a tinkerer, an inventor, you know. Have you ever heard of the staple remover? The salad spinner?"

Addie said, "Wait…you invented those?"

She thought it was more likely he was an inventor of stories.

"Well, I did, but I didn't get credit for them. I was coming up with a formula for superglue too, but someone else beat me to it." He finished the bag of chips and made a face. "Can't anyone make a plain old potato chip anymore?" he grumbled. "And that's another thing. The food here is terrible. Breakfast is the worst. Limp toast and coffee-colored water! And I really miss my stewed prunes. No one knows how to make stewed prunes anymore."

Addie had never heard of them before, and they sounded terrible, but that was beside the point.

"Stewed prunes?" she said. "My mom makes great stewed prunes! She's the best prune stewer ever!"

The things she had to do to help Tish keep her job.

Brad's deep voice and Dickson's squeaky voice were coming toward them.

The old man glared at her. He could hear Brad and Dickson too.

"I hate being here," he growled, "and I suspect you're lying, but if I could get some decent stewed prunes, then maybe the month wouldn't be a complete disaster."

Brad's tall shape filled the doorway.

"Wow, there you are, Mr. Norris! Gee, you know everyone's looking for you?"

CHAPTER 4

Melinda Sloat was the proud president and chief executive officer of Happy Valley Village Retirement Community. It was her job to keep an eye on everyone and everything. And she was really good at her job. If she wasn't in her glass-walled office off the atrium at the main entrance, she was popping up for a surprise inspection of a food prep station, a nurse's office, or the staff break room. On her very, very high heels and holding her megamug of coffee, she was in a perpetual state of nastiness.

The only thing that gave her any enjoyment was thinking up better ways to sell and market HVV. She came up with all of HVV's sales pitches herself: "Gracious Living in the Golden Age of Retirement," "Join Our Vibrant Community on 85 Acres," "Reservations Taken Now for Your Next Exciting Chapter!," and her latest, which gave her tingles every time she saw it,

"Home with a Heart," where the *o* in *Home* was a bright red heart.

She was most creative during her monthly appointments at the Cut Above hair salon (she wouldn't have been caught dead at Lulu's House of Hair). Making sure her blond hair retained that natural, sun-kissed look took four hours. She always came up with one or two new ideas as she blissfully whiled away the time with soaps, chemicals, foils, hot air, and magazines.

She wasn't the only one who loved her hair appointments. Everyone at HVV felt her absence and breathed a breezy, facility-wide sigh of relief. Staff and residents took time to laugh with one another. The chef didn't measure how many ounces of butter he added to the cream sauce. Wilma sat down and watched WWE wrestling on TV with Dickson. Mrs. Firillo let her little dog off her leash.

❋

The next day was one of those days when Mrs. Sloat would be gone all afternoon. Addie hadn't even met her yet, but even she felt more relaxed and happy as she waved goodbye to a few of her new friends and left school.

Until she found Dickson waiting for her around the corner of the school building.

"Is anyone following you?" he asked, pushing his glasses up his nose.

She looked around.

"No, why would anyone follow me?"

He let his breath out and started walking away.

"There was a problem at lunch and some kids said they were going to get me after school."

Addie walked behind him.

"Is that why you've got pizza sauce down your pants?"

"Just let me know if you see anyone behind us."

There was no one, and, even if there had been, Addie had taken care of a bully or two.

"You should do what I do," she said, still in a good mood.

Dickson stopped and turned to look at her.

"So, first, you eat at the nut-free table at lunch."

"But I'm not allergic to nuts."

"Who cares? You just tell them you are. The nut-free table usually has only one or two kids, and the teachers keep an eye on you so you won't die or something. So those kids probably wouldn't get away with bothering you."

Dickson walked on.

"But I like nuts," he muttered.

"Then, at recess, you stay on the swings, play basketball, or hit the monkey bars. If you're busy, kids won't notice you as much to pick on you. And hey, you might find a friend or two. It's always worked for me."

Dickson gave a grunt.

"Okay for you if you like those things, but I don't."

"Well, that's all the school survival skills I know. Hey, I know one thing, remember we heard Mrs. Sloat is gone this afternoon?"

That did the trick. Dickson brightened right up and started to skip down the path.

By the time Wilma opened the door, he was ready to rush right past her.

"Hey, how about a nice 'Hello, Wilma!' before anything else?"

"Hello, Wilma," they both said.

"That's better. Dickson, what is that on your nice clothes? Was it those same kids again?" Wilma looked like a thunderstorm but then let it pass with a loud sigh. "Hey, Addie, your mom said she wants to see you about something, but I think she's taking Mr. Norris for a walk right now."

"Wait," said Addie, "my mom has to take Mr. Norris for a walk?"

"Yeah, honey, no one else volunteered. They ought to be back soon...if they both survive," she added under her breath.

"Come on, Addie," said Dickson, "while it's quiet, follow me!"

He led the way down the carpeted hall, the one that looked like a fancy hotel, past doors of residents' rooms, to where it widened out into a lounge. There were comfortable chairs, a sofa, and a giant TV, with doors leading out to a terrace. Off to one side were a dining room and a nurses' station. Then, as if the lounge area was an elbow between two parts of an arm, another hall of rooms went off at an angle.

After Dickson waved to the aide on duty and some women playing cards in the dining room, he showed Addie where to leave her backpack.

"Okay, first things first. Miss Trotter's, then a tour. Better bring your map notebook. I have a lot to show you."

He headed down the other hall past one door after another. "We're going to go to the end and start from there." Most of the doors were slightly ajar. Faint sounds of radios or televisions trickled out of the rooms. Several doorways had trays outside them on the floor. Addie saw containers of half-eaten applesauce, plastic-wrapped crackers, spilled soup. She was thinking the whole place had a smell about it of stale, leftover food when Dickson stopped in front of her, waving toward the elevator and stairs signs.

"That goes to the main building, but this," he said, turning back and spreading his hands out in front of him, "is Arborvine. The best hallway in the whole place! It's the part of HVV that is assisted living...you know, where people live if they need extra help with things. Addie, are you listening?"

No, she wasn't. She was staring at an old man in a wheelchair parked in the first doorway. Dickson said, "Oh, hi, Mr. Greenberg. This is Addie."

The sign on the door said MALCOLM GREENBERG. He gave no sign of hearing or seeing them. His eyes stared straight ahead, his head sunk in a neck brace. He didn't move. If his eyes hadn't been open, Addie thought he could've been dead already.

Dickson whispered to her. "He doesn't talk. I don't know if he understands anything."

Dickson went on to the next door, which read CYNTHIA TROTTER.

"Miss Trotter is the best! It's like Halloween all year long."

Outside the door was an old-fashioned child's rocking chair on which five dolls sat bunched together, one with a little parasol. The way their china eyes stared ahead looked like their neighbor, Mr. Greenberg, sitting ten feet away, only the dolls with their rosy cheeks and painted smiles looked a lot more alive. At the dolls' feet, on an antique embroidered stool, a moth-eaten lion lay next to a monkey missing an ear. A small table completed the display. On top of a lace cloth sat a dolls' tea set and a dish of candy in wrappers.

"She fills it every morning, but we're only supposed to take two each. See the sign?"

A small white card lay beside the candy dish. In wispy writing, it said, *One for now, one for later. That's all you get, Alligator!*

After they took their two candies each, Dickson took her to the next door, which had MINERVA SWIFT written in big, bold red letters on the sign. There was a shiny red electric scooter, like a motorized chair on wheels, parked near the half-open door. The basket on the front of the scooter was packed with books. Addie could hear a bird chirping in the room, along with a TV. She started to peek inside, but Dickson caught her arm.

"Wait," he said, "Ms. Swift hates visitors while she's watching the news. And I mean HATES! You can meet her later. Come meet Mrs. Firillo."

They were almost back at the lounge now. Wilma came by with a tray of medications.

"How's the tour going? Have you seen your mom yet, Addie?" She looked toward the terrace door. "I wonder where they are. I hope we don't have to go looking for Mr. Norris again like yesterday." Wilma shook her head. "What a mess that was!

"You know, honey," she said in a low voice, "it's always the newest person working as a companion who gets the hardest job. I think Mrs. Sloat likes to see if they can take it. Let's hope your mom can manage. She looks like she has some spunk to her... like you do too, am I right?" She laughed.

Yeah, spunk. Maybe it ran in the family. Granny Lu had enough for her whole family, enough for all of Mount Repose, Maine, for that matter. If Granny Lu had been at HVV, Addie thought she would enjoy getting these old-sters dolled up and whipped into shape.

"Is Mrs. Firillo in her room?" Dickson asked.

"I think she's outside giving Izzy a walk before din-ner," said Wilma. "That's right, Addie hasn't met the Plant Lady yet."

Addie had noticed a doorway with vines snaking out of a room and over the door.

"Then let's go next door and see Mr. Trippling," said

Dickson. Addie hurried to draw in her map notebook. She was losing track of all these old geezers.

"See you in a bit," said Wilma. "I'm off to Mr. Greenberg's."

Dickson stopped at the next door, just before the lounge.

"Mr. Trippling and Mrs. Firillo sort of like each other and sort of hate each other at the same time. He gets mad about all her plants, and she gets tired of his opera, but underneath I think they really like each other. They practice speaking Italian together. It's pretty funny."

Dickson knocked on the door, which was partway open.

"Yes?"

They went in.

A man was standing in front of the large window of his room. He turned.

"Hello, Dickson. Will you look at that Patsy Firillo out there?" he said, turning back to the window. "It's cold and damp and she's out there with no coat or hat or boots on. But, of course, she has to put a silly sweater on that dog of hers!"

All three of them looked out the window. Mrs. Firillo saw them and waved gaily. She scooped up a little terrier and waved one of her paws up and down at them.

Mr. Trippling cleared his throat with a humph.

"That woman," he said, shaking his head and turning to them.

"Well, Dickson, who is this?"

Mr. Trippling wasn't much taller than Addie, but he

straightened up as tall as he could go, as if he could still hear his mother telling him to stand up straight. His hair and skin were exactly the same color of pale, and he wore a bright yellow bow tie.

"This is Addie. Her mother works here now as a companion."

Mr. Trippling held out his hand and shook Addie's.

"Nice to meet you," he said formally, with a hint of a bow.

"Mr. Trippling gets me to show him things on his computer," said Dickson. "He was trying to do it all himself. Remember, Mr. Trippling, when you were trying to print out that whole online manual and it was a hundred pages? And then you wanted to order some earmuffs, but you got thirty-two of them by mistake?"

Mr. Trippling smiled weakly at Addie.

"I just can't seem to get the hang of it, and sometimes I get so anxious about which button to push I have to go lie down. I don't know what I'd do without Dickson. Which reminds me, I wrote down a question for you. It's here somewhere. It's about a message that popped up in one of those things you call windows." He bent over his desk.

The two of them got busy at the computer, so Addie decided it was time to edge out of the room.

She was just settling down on the sofa in the lounge to draw a map of Arborvine when her mother came down the hall.

Tish dropped onto the sofa next to Addie and let out a deep breath.

"What a day!" she said, resting her head back on the cushions and closing her eyes. Addie leaned closer to pull Tish's sleeves down. After the job interview, Tish had told her that Mrs. Sloat had said she never wanted to see the tattoos. Ever. Or the nose ring. Or the hair tinsel.

Her mom suddenly sat up and turned to her.

"By the way, who told Mr. Norris I could stew prunes? I've been stalling him all day, but I've got to bring him some tomorrow morning!"

CHAPTER 5

Wilma came to the rescue.

"Ask Desmond. He'll be here soon bringing the residents their dinner. If anyone knows about stewed prunes, he will."

Dickson appeared at Wilma's elbow.

"Des can do anything. He even fixed Mr. Trippling's printer!"

"Well, he would be a lifesaver," said Tish. "Hey, are you Dickson? Thanks for showing Addie around." She tried to ruffle his hair, but he ducked away. "Addie says you're into WWE. Way to go!" She struck a pose that might have been a wrestling pose, Addie wasn't sure.

"Addie, can you hang out here for another minute? I have to see if Mr. Norris wants his dinner in his room or the dining room."

As the clock in the nurses' station got closer to five, Arborvine came to life for dinnertime. The ladies in the dining room packed up their cards and wandered into the lounge.

Dickson started to introduce them.

"This is..."

A woman with bright red lipstick took over.

"Everyone calls us A, B, C, D," she said, sticking out her hand to Addie. "The Mrs. Abernathy, Binterhoffer, Cohen, and Dunn. We sound like a law firm, don't we, girls?"

They burst into a round of "we've-heard-it-before-but-it's-still-a-good-one" giggles.

Mrs. B came close to Addie.

"And your poor mother's the one who has to take care of...THAT MAN!"

It looked like they had plenty more to say on the subject, but at that moment Mrs. Firillo blew in the terrace door with her dog in her arms.

"Oh, Patsy and Izzy!" said Mrs. A.

Mrs. Firillo was shaking her head.

"I'm so worried, dearie. Izzy hasn't pooped all day."

Everyone looked at Izzy, a brown-and-white terrier that never seemed to stop squirming and wriggling.

Mr. Trippling stepped out of his room, dressed for dinner in a jacket and bow tie.

"Hello, Gene. Did you know Izzy was constipated?" said Mrs. D.

"That's a nasty business," he said. "I've been suffering from a bit of that myself."

"Okay, everyone," said Wilma, joining the throng. "Here's Des with the cart, so let's all move into the dining room to give him some space."

"I better go and wait for my mother," said Dickson, getting his backpack. "See you tomorrow, Addie!"

Other residents wandered in and took their seats. A woman in a full-length evening dress and fur jacket went up to Wilma.

"Is the captain dining with us tonight, Wilma?"

Wilma guided her to a table.

"He said he was sorry, Mrs. Ruckleshaus, but he can't make it tonight. Maybe tomorrow."

"I'm sure he's got a million things to do. Maybe I'll see him at the lifeboat drill tomorrow."

Wilma nodded. "Mmm-hmm."

She came and whispered to Addie.

"Isn't Mrs. Ruckleshaus something? Ninety years old and the happiest person I know. She was a showgirl back on Broadway and now she thinks she's on a cruise."

Okay, thought Addie, now she was sure Granny Lu would have loved this place.

Aides and companions handed out dinner trays. A frail woman using a walker crept out of Miss Trotter's room, so Addie guessed it was Miss Trotter herself. She snuck quietly into her seat. A companion took a tray down the hall toward Mr. Greenberg.

Tish got Mr. Norris's dinner tray.

"Let me get him set up in his room," she said to Addie, "and then I'll be right back. Don't let Des get away before we see him."

Des was taller than Wilma when they stood side by side. Wilma caught Addie's eye.

"Desmond is my nephew," she said, giving him a

squeeze. "Isn't he a fine-looking young man?" Des rolled his eyes. "He's in the culinary arts program at the local college." She looked at him, her eyes shining. "He's going to be an amazing chef one day."

Des smiled, embarrassed, and went to hand out the last tray.

He was moving the cart when Tish came back down the hall.

"Mr. Norris is all set, so I'm done! Whew! Des, I am desperate and need your help." She put her hands together like she was praying. "Please, please, please tell me you know how to stew prunes. Mr. Norris wants some by tomorrow morning and I promised I'd make him some."

Des looked at her and gave her a big grin.

"Wow, that's something I don't get asked every day. But sure, not a problem. Only, I can't do it now while dinner's going on. Can you come to the kitchen after eight o'clock? That's when it's quiet and we'll have the place to ourselves."

Tish thought a minute.

"Yeah," she said, looking at Addie. "Yeah, we can hang out here till then. Thanks, Des."

⁕

"Crazy Aunt Tina's ready to kill me for missing dinner," said Tish after finishing the phone call. They were standing by the elevators. "She was cooking something special. Or so she said." Tish leaned against the wall with her phone in her hand.

Tish referred to her brother as Nice Uncle Tim because he was. Everyone liked him. He was the youngest of her brothers, the closest one in age to Tish. When he was eighteen, he'd gone into the army, where he met Tina. They both served eight years, then married and moved to Pennsylvania to be near her family. Tim went to work for his father-in-law, a general contractor, and Tina worked as a bookkeeper and was studying to be an accountant. With their two kids, Bella and Logan, the little house was pretty busy, but "Crazy Aunt Tina" was super organized and responsible and managed the lives of everyone. She was only "crazy" because Tish, being the exact opposite, made her that way.

Addie leaned against the wall next to Tish.

"I wish we could get our own place," she said. "I like Bella, but she really wants her bedroom back. Either that or she wants to sleep with us because she says Logan makes too much noise."

"Yeah, I know," said Tish, "but that's not going to happen, is it, until I can make some money."

A red scooter whirred around the corner and squeaked to a stop.

"Hi, Ms. Swift," said Tish, straightening up. "Here, let me get the button for you. We're going up too."

The woman on the scooter gave them a wintry smile and a "Thank you." She used the time waiting for the elevator to pin up hair that had escaped from the nest on her head.

"This is my daughter, Addie. Short for Adelaide."

The woman looked over at Addie.

"Adelaide. Now that's a name you don't hear very often. I think it's old German by way of French. How do you do, Adelaide? My name is Minerva, after the Roman goddess of wisdom. I have a theory that interesting people have interesting names. Are you interesting?"

After taking a moment to think about it, Addie said, "I'm kind of working on it."

"Good answer," said Minerva Swift. "I'm working on it too."

Upstairs, Ms. Swift peeled off to go meet friends in the main dining room, while Addie and her mother went to the employees' cafeteria.

"I bet this is way better than what Aunt Tina was making for dinner," said Addie as they went down the cafeteria line. She loaded up on fried fish fillets with lemon wedges and tartar sauce, mashed potatoes, salad, and blueberry cheesecake for dessert.

"You know what I think we should do after dinner?" said Tish. She had a certain gleam in her eyes that Addie wasn't sure about.

"Everybody's at dinner and then they all go to bed. We have at least two hours before we can meet Des, so... let's go exploring."

CHAPTER 6

"Hi!" Tish gave the security guard at the reception desk her best spotlight-bright smile as they passed by him. The main entrance was an impressive eight-sided atrium sweeping up to skylights high overhead in the ceiling. With her ID badge around her neck, Tish looked official. The guard gave her a routine smile in return. The badge also meant she could get through almost any locked door by holding it up to the door sensors.

Addie followed her down a curving stairway lined with plants to the basement level. Tish was right. There was no one around.

"This is going to be fun," Tish said. "I haven't been down here at all."

She pulled out a handful of mints from her pocket and gave half to Addie.

"They have a big bowl of these by the main dining room. Cool, huh?"

"How come there are different dining rooms?"

"The main one is for people who live on their own in apartments. The dining room at Arborvine is for people like Mr. Norris who need help with stuff like walking or dressing. And there are more dining rooms I haven't even seen yet. Wow, look at that!"

The sign on the door said MINIATURE TRAINS. They peeked through the window, but it was dark inside.

"Wait," said Addie, "you have to get Mr. Norris dressed?"

"Not so far! That would be something, let me tell you. No, he manages on his own." Tish held her badge up to the door.

"Mom, are you sure it's okay to go in?"

"Yeah, why not?" The door clicked and Tish pulled it open.

She flicked on the light switch inside the door.

"Wow, this is crazy! It's like the Santa's Village we used to go see at Christmas!"

There were little green hills with trees and a pretend river winding its way between them. Train tracks ran through tunnels in the mountains. There were sheep in mountain meadows and a tiny village with a clock tower and a flower market.

"We have GOT to bring Bella and Logan here," said Addie. "They would go nuts over this."

"Do you see where to turn it on?" said Tish, looking around.

"Tish, really, I don't think that's a great idea. If

something went wrong… You said Mrs. Sloat was going to look for any reason not to keep you."

"Okay, okay, I can't see a switch anyway. But someday we're coming back here."

They went on through HVV's lower level, peeking through the windows of the bank, the carpentry shop, the art studio, and the hair and nail salon.

"It's like a whole Old People City down here," said Tish, walking by the post office and the library.

"Hey, look at the gym!" said Addie. "Granny Lu would have loved that!"

"Wouldn't she?"

There was a squishy sound of sneakers along with clinks and jingles, and sure enough, Brad rounded the corner.

"Hey, ladies!" he said, putting his badge with all his keys up to the gym door. "Having fun? I forgot something in here I need for tomorrow." He turned on a row of switches and the gym was suddenly bright as day. "Come on in and look around."

"We were just saying," said Tish, "how much my mom would have loved this place. She was an exercise nut. Right, Addie?"

"Yeah, we did all the TV shows: yoga, steps, Zumba, Bollywood."

"Really!" said Brad. He picked up a folder from his desk. "Impressive. Oh, Tish, before I forget, I know Mr. Norris complains a lot, but he actually sounded pleased that you took him for a walk today to his old house. He said the nurses had told him it was too far. I've got to hand it to you, you seem to be able to handle him."

"Well, thanks," Tish said. "That's nice to hear. I'm sure he'd never tell me."

"You know, I'd love to know more about him," Brad said. "He's a big man, but he moves in that fluid way that athletes do. There's got to be a story there somewhere. He blew me away this morning when he lifted weights. You should have seen him. None of the other residents can lift as much as he can. I'd love to see what he could do if he let me work with him regularly."

Tish nodded.

"He says he's strong enough. He just wants to get his balance back so he won't fall. We can both work on him!"

Brad laughed.

"As much as he'll let us. Well, that's it for me."

Brad turned off the lights as they went out.

"You ladies have a good night," he called over his shoulder.

Tish checked her phone.

"We still have time. Ooo," she said, seeing a door at the end of the hall. "That's what we want." It said POOL.

As they got closer, Addie could smell the chlorine.

With Tish's badge and a click, they were in. The air was thick and heavy and warm. It lay on Addie's skin like an extra blanket. Two dim security lights shone on the big blue swimming pool, which was so still and calm it looked like a sheet of plastic.

"Super cool, huh?" whispered Tish.

Off to the side was another little pool.

Tish shook Addie and squealed.

"A hot tub! Take off your shoes!"

"Mom..."

But Tish was already at the control panel on the wall, eyeing the buttons.

A motor switched on and churned the water up into a rolling froth. Tish ran over, kicked off her shoes, and sat on the side of the pool with her legs in the water.

"Ahh, got to live it up while we can, right?" she said. "Wish I had my bathing suit."

Addie went and sat next to her. She had to admit it was pretty great.

Light reflecting from the water flickered blue over the walls and ceiling. It was calming and peaceful.

"So, how is it with Mr. Norris?" Addie asked.

"Oh, you know." Tish shrugged. "I bother him, but then everyone bothers him. And some of his nasty remarks about this place, especially about Mrs. Sloat, are hilarious."

They stared at the water.

"Interesting what Brad said," said Tish. "About Mr. Norris being an athlete and lifting weights. I wonder what he used to do...whether he was in some sport or something. His family must have been rich to own this whole place." She made circles in the water with her feet.

"We walked over to his house today, went through a few of the rooms downstairs. Nothing too exciting, but there's a big old garage next door that he didn't want to go in. He said no one was allowed in but him." Tish sighed. "A man of mystery. Which only makes me more curious."

She checked her phone.

"Time for kitchen duty."

*

They found Des wiping down the big stainless steel counters in the industrial-sized kitchen. Two employees were on the other side of the kitchen doing the same thing.

"Hey, good timing. I'm almost done."

While he finished, Addie snooped around, peeking into the employees' cafeteria where they'd eaten dinner, the lunchroom for the residents, the snack shop, and the large main dining room. It was so big and dark she had trouble seeing where it ended. Happy Valley Village seemed to be growing bigger by the minute, and if she didn't start on a map soon, she might never get it done.

As she came back into the kitchen, Des thumped a big bag onto the counter.

"Okay, prunes," he said.

"Okay, prunes!" said Tish.

He cut open the bag.

"Hey, so far, so good," said Tish. "I can do that!"

Des laughed.

"It's really not hard. Not too many people want stewed prunes anymore, but we keep some on hand just in case." He handed one to Addie and one to Tish.

Addie looked at the wrinkled brown lump in her hand.

"It looks like a supersized raisin," she said.

Tish looked at hers and made a face before taking a bite.

"Well, it tastes good, anyway."

"They're just plums, you know," said Des, dropping a handful into a pot, adding a squeeze of lemon, and covering them with water.

"That's about it. The lemon's a nice touch but not absolutely necessary. Cook them slowly at a simmer for twenty or thirty minutes. And they're done. Keep them in the fridge. Easy peasy."

"Well, if I can't do that, I'm really hopeless," said Tish.

"And if he wants to special order them," said Des, "talk to the dining department."

"All right, but I'm thinking for the first few mornings, it would be good if I cook them to make sure he gets them...hopefully the way he wants them."

"Well, let me know if I can help," said Des. "I have classes in the morning, but I'm usually hanging around the kitchen or over at Arborvine later in the day because that's where I'm assigned. I don't mind doing special things for the residents if I have time."

"Thanks, Des. I really appreciate it."

"No problem," he said. "I like messing around in a kitchen and making something people will enjoy."

When the prunes were done, Des showed them the pot.

"So that's what stewed prunes look like?" said Addie.

Tish shook her head and laughed.

"Looks like something you'd see in a toilet!"

CHAPTER 7

The only person at Happy Valley Village who wasn't scared of Melinda Sloat, or the Sloat, as she was known in whispers, was Dr. Alan Barker, head of the HVV Residents' Association. He had run a large naval hospital before retiring and moving to HVV with his wife. His job, as he saw it, was to make sure every resident did their part in following the HVV Rules and Regulations in order to optimize (one of his favorite words) harmonious (another favorite word) living for all. He and Mrs. Sloat got along really well. She considered Dr. Barker and his wife, Genevieve, to be exactly the kind of people HVV needed more of, which was why she put their photograph in every sales brochure.

The Barkers had been living in one of HVV's fancier "Country Estate" townhomes, but when Genevieve Barker got pneumonia, she was moved first to the nursing wing and, as she got better, Arborvine was the next step for her to recuperate. Because the Barkers were such important people, it was a big day when they came to Arborvine. Mrs. Sloat had alerted the nurses and staff that everything must be perfect. She was personally escorting Genevieve Barker to her new room. Dr. Barker would stay in their townhome but intended to visit his wife regularly.

Mrs. Barker's arrival happened when Addie was picking out four pieces of candy from Miss Trotter's candy dish for herself and Dickson, who'd stayed downstairs in Mrs. Firillo's storage compartment deep in his WWE magazine. She settled a doll that had fallen off the rocking chair. She gave an awkward wave to Mr. Greenberg next door in his wheelchair, but he was doing his usual stiff-as-a-mummy thing. She checked on Mrs. A, B, C, and D to see who was winning the bridge game. Afternoons on Arborvine were becoming familiar—even the smell was starting to feel homey and comfortable.

She was talking to Mrs. Firillo and playing with Izzy in the lounge when Wilma, clicking buttons on the TV remote, looked down the hall.

"Uh-oh, here comes trouble," she said in a low voice.

Mrs. Firillo scooped up Izzy and disappeared into her room. Mr. Trippling left the jigsaw puzzle he was working on and closed his door. Mrs. Ruckleshaus put down her magazine, grabbed her life preserver, and made off down the hall.

Addie hadn't met Mrs. Sloat yet, but something about the blond woman approaching with a man pushing a woman in a wheelchair gave her the shivers. She snuck the candies into her pocket and stood still.

"Who does this girl belong to?" called the blond woman, still thirty feet away but focused on Addie.

Wilma stepped forward.

"This is Addie Munroe, Mrs. Sloat. Her mother is Tish Munroe, the new companion. She's only here for a minute. Tish gets off work soon. Say hello to Mrs. Sloat, Addie." She gave Addie a little nudge.

Mrs. Sloat eyed Addie. She did not look pleased.

"Well, nice to meet you," said Mrs. Sloat. "Now go wherever you need to go." She turned to Wilma and whispered, "Is he around? Norris?"

"He went out for a walk. With Tish." Wilma winked at Addie.

"Thank God," breathed Mrs. Sloat. She turned to the man behind her. "Let's go see this wonderful room we have for you. It has the very best view of the...the..."

"The greenery," said Wilma.

"That's right, the greenery," said Mrs. Sloat. "Wilma, you know Dr. and Mrs. Barker, don't you? Of course you do. Dr. Barker has been head of our residents' association for how many years now, Alan? And we're so happy to have his lovely wife, Genevieve, staying with us on Arborvine while she gets her strength back."

Mrs. Barker smiled a sweet, nervous little smile and held on to her pearls.

They moved down the hall and turned into a room.

"Right next to Mr. Norris," said Wilma. "Oh, boy."

With that, the door to the terrace slammed open. In a gust of swirling leaves, Mr. Norris banged and crashed his walker, trying to get it through the door. Tish was right behind him, but there wasn't enough room for her to get through the door to untangle the walker.

"BLOODY CONTRAPTION!" he yelled. "Who the hell designed these doors so no one can get through them!" With a final kick, the walker ended up on its side across the room, wheels spinning.

"There, you take care of it since you think it's so wonderful," he snapped at Tish. Then he saw Addie. He pressed his lips together. "Hmmph! What are you looking at?"

Mrs. Sloat came quickly down the hall the way very important women walk in very high heels. She meant business.

"Is there a problem?"

"Ha! There you are!" Mr. Norris glared at her. "I will not use this piece of junk to go out for a walk. It only gets in the way and makes me fall!"

Mrs. Sloat eyed Tish.

"Did Mr. Norris fall?"

"Why don't you ask me, for Pete's sake? I'm standing right here! No, I did not fall. Absolutely not."

"But...," said Tish, looking between Mr. Norris and Mrs. Sloat. "Something happened. I'm not sure. Mr. Norris had a coughing spell and—"

"For crying out loud, it was just a cough!"

"But somehow," Tish continued, "we both ended up on the ground." She looked at Mrs. Sloat. "I could have bumped into him. I don't know for sure what happened. It all happened so fast."

"Everything okay here?" said Dr. Barker, joining in with a smile.

"I did not FALL!" shouted Mr. Norris.

Mrs. Sloat was as stiff and angry as her sprayed hair. She was trying to look calm and professional for Dr. Barker and deal with Mr. Norris at the same time.

"Mr. Norris, we are only interested in your safety and well-being. You know we all have to make minor adjustments when we follow doctors' orders." Her soothing voice was like cough syrup.

"Exactly," said Dr. Barker.

Mr. Norris relocated his deep, dark eyes onto Dr. Barker and studied him as if he was some peculiar life-form.

"Bunch of CRAP!" spat Mr. Norris.

Mrs. Sloat tried a different tack.

"Your doctors will be pleased to hear you're making an effort. I hope your companion is making sure you go for walks and get to the gym every day? You know I'll be looking at your progress report and for your feedback on her work."

Tish couldn't have been any closer, but Mrs. Sloat talked about her as if she wasn't there. Addie could tell from her tight lips that her mother was fuming.

Mr. Norris leaned toward Mrs. Sloat.

"Well, Mrs. Sloat, for your information, this woman is doing her best to put up with me. Actually, she's doing an excellent job. Why"—he looked at Addie with a wicked gleam—"she even brings me stewed prunes! She and I both have a month to prove ourselves, as you well know, Mrs. Sloat. A month! I have no idea why she wants to stay here, whereas I...I cannot wait to LEAVE!"

CHAPTER 8

I t was totally weird!"

Tish was on her break. She and Addie sat at a corner table in the employees' cafeteria. Addie had a big mug of hot chocolate with marshmallows in front of her; her mom had a coffee.

"One minute we were walking along just fine," said Tish. "Mr. Norris hates his walker, but I'd talked him into trying it. We'd gone all the way to his old house and back. Then he started to cough. And I mean cough! Huge, rattling coughs and big gulps of air that caught him off-balance. I've never heard anyone cough like that. I was getting my phone out to call the nurse when he slammed into me, and the next thing I knew we were both flat on our backs!"

"Mrs. Sloat looked like she was going to detonate."

"Was that the first time you'd seen her? She was just being her usual witchy self."

"But then Mr. Norris told her you were doing a good job!"

Tish laughed.

"You never know, do you? He can be full of surprises." She finished her coffee.

"Hey, sorry about tonight. Hope you don't mind. With this concert they're having, they're short-handed and asked me to stay with Genevieve Barker. It's her first night at Arborvine, and Mr. Norris isn't going to it, so he doesn't need me. Plus it means overtime pay." She smoothed Addie's hair. "Can you find something to do for a few hours?"

"Tish, really, it's fine. Can we get dinner here in the cafeteria again? It's so fun getting whatever I want. And I wouldn't mind getting out of bedtime with Bella and Logan for once. Ever since I started reading bedtime stories to Bella and doing funny voices, she won't let me stop. After a while, you know, talking like Thomas the Tank Engine kind of gets to you."

Tish laughed and waggled a finger at her.

"The trouble is, you're so good at it." She looked down at her coffee. "But I hear you. I can miss one night of Aunt Tina singing 'Little Bunny Foo Foo' to Logan. That has got to be the all-time worst children's song ever!"

When they got back to Arborvine, Des was stacking the dinner trays in his cart and the residents were heading to the auditorium in the main building. Gene Trippling was outside his door straightening his bow tie.

"Patsy, hurry up or we'll be late," he called, pushing the vines in her doorway aside.

"I'm coming," said Mrs. Firillo. "I'm trying to find a radio station Izzy will like while I'm gone."

Mrs. A, B, C, and D were going off in a cluster, holding one another's arms for comfort and support.

They couldn't remember whether the concert was a piano or a string quartet, and which composer it was—Bach, Brahms, Berlioz, or Bartók—but they knew it started with a B.

Minerva Swift revved up her red scooter and took off, riding next to Mrs. Ruckleshaus, who was wearing a long evening dress of sequins and lace.

Wilma called out after them,

"Mrs. Ruckleshaus, say hello to the captain!"

"Oh, I will, chérie! I'm sure he'll be there with the other officers. Although," she said, giving Wilma a troubled look, "I don't do well in a dark theater if the ship starts to roll." She patted her stomach.

Wilma chuckled.

"I wouldn't worry. Sea's supposed to be calm tonight."

With her walker, Cynthia Trotter brought up the rear, following a companion wheeling Mr. Greenberg.

When they had gone, Arborvine returned to its quiet, sleepy self.

"Okay, folks," said Wilma, reaching for the remote. "Time for some excitement! Let's see if we can find some WWE!"

She'd been trying to cheer Dickson up all afternoon. He was balled up at one end of the sofa in the lounge. Earlier at school, he'd been shoved under the lunch table again by Marshall, the school bully of bullies. Addie and

Wilma kept finding bits of sticky substances to pull off him. "Next time," Addie had told him on the walk from school, "think twice about taking a slug in a sock for Science Show-and-Tell Day."

"Someday the world will appreciate the finer points of slug slime!" was all he could mutter.

Addie lost interest in the TV wrestling show in less than a minute. She pulled out her map notebook and curled up in an easy chair on the other side of the lounge. She was finishing a diagram of Arborvine, showing who lived where, when, down the hall, she saw Mr. Norris sneak out of his room. With his two canes, he crept quietly away toward the stairs Addie had gone down her first day at HVV.

Wilma and Dickson were so busy with a big takedown move known as the T-Rex Tickle, they never saw her leave. She snuck down the hall, past the closed door to Genevieve Barker's room where Tish was, and followed Mr. Norris.

He never looked around once along the hallway of storage compartments. It was like he was on a mission. But then he came to the elevators and stopped.

"Are you following me?" he said without turning around.

Addie thought she hadn't made a sound.

"Are you trying to escape again? Because if you are, my mom is going to get in trouble."

"I'm resigned to my month's detention," he said, rolling his eyes upward. "But I thought an evening visit to the gym wouldn't hurt. The sooner I'm steadier on my feet, the sooner I can exit this place...only I'm not sure how to get there from here."

"Okay then, so this is where I come in." Addie opened her notebook. "See? This is exactly why I draw maps."

Mr. Norris grumbled but followed her as they took the elevator up one flight to another basement level and walked down long hallways to the gym. It was locked.

She waited while Mr. Norris rattled and shook the doors anyway. When he had about given up, she pointed to a sign on the glass.

"Looks like Brad closes up at five p.m. on Fridays."

With an angry growl, Mr. Norris raised one of his gold-topped canes toward the glass door. "Why do I have to fit my schedule around theirs?"

"Of course, there's another answer," she said quickly.

"Besides breaking in?" He paused. "Well, spit it out, then!"

"Follow me," she said, turning to another page of her notebook.

She led him down in another elevator to a subbasement hallway where they were in the warm, throbbing heart of the heating and plumbing department of HVV. Furnaces hummed behind closed doors. Pipes above them gurgled and clanked.

"There you go," Addie said, pointing down the hallway. Before it came to a dead end, the hall was lined with stuff.

"Where in blazes are we?"

"Dickson says they call this the Come and Get It.

People leave things they don't want, and other people take them. And here is an almost-like-new treadmill."

And there one was, wedged in between chairs, bookcases, exercise balls, standing lamps, and toaster ovens.

"I don't think..." Mr. Norris was turning away.

Addie caught one of his canes to stop him.

"You know you're not going to get better if you don't exercise more, right? Haven't you heard of 'use it or lose it'? Now, there was one time when Ms. Schmidt's husband died and she didn't do anything, I mean anything, for weeks and weeks. Granny Lu finally went and picked her up, brought her in for a new hairdo, gave her a pair of bright orange leggings, and got her hooked on TV exercise shows. Well, you should have seen Ms. Schmidt a month later. As Granny Lu said, 'she was a sight to see'—and I mean that in a good way."

He growled at her. "Here, take these," he said, shoving his canes at her, "and show me how to turn this blasted thing on."

"So, you push the start button. Granny Lu always liked this workout here, but you can pick whatever you want. Make sure you hold on, though. And this is the stop button. Okay?" The treadmill started to move. He plodded slowly. She watched him for a few minutes.

"Look, I've got to go pee. Keep holding on, and I'll be back in a minute." She laid his canes on the floor nearby. "Will you be all right?"

"Of course I'll be all right! All I'm doing is walking, for heaven's sakes!"

Addie went off. It took her a while to find a bathroom

in the maze of basements and elevators. When she got back, she found him sitting on the side of the treadmill. He was wiping his face with a handkerchief.

"Are you okay?"

He nodded. "I'm fine...had a good walk."

She checked the controls on the treadmill.

"Wait a minute," she said. "It says you went fifty-five miles! What buttons were you pushing?"

He waved a hand.

"How should I know? Thing must be broken like the other crap down here." He picked up his canes. "Help me up. There's somewhere I want to go while everyone's at that silly concert."

CHAPTER 9

"Can you get me into the old house? The original part before they stuck on that disgusting atrium and entrance?"

Mr. Norris teetered a bit on his canes. He looked recovered from the treadmill, but Addie wasn't sure if they should go anywhere. The reading of fifty-five miles on the treadmill bothered her, but really, when she thought about it, if he'd truly gone fifty-five miles, which was impossible, he'd be dead by now. So the treadmill had to be broken, just like Mr. Norris said. Or he'd gone crazy pushing buttons, or something.

His black eyes glittered.

"Hurry up," he said, taking off in the wrong direction. "What are you waiting for?"

She caught up to him and showed him one of her newest maps.

"It isn't finished yet. But it's this way, I think," she said, pointing in the opposite direction.

Addie led the way up in one set of elevators, down a deserted hall, out one door, across an enclosed garden, in another door, up in another elevator, and down another hall. Then she stopped.

"What now?" said Mr. Norris.

They were at an intersection of four hallways.

"I don't know," she said. "This is beyond what I've put on my map."

Both of them turned in circles, peering in every direction. Addie didn't like this at all.

Mr. Norris, however, was looking brighter.

"Aha, this is what is called Terra Incognita, or Unknown Territory. Where's your sense of adventure?" He pointed with his cane. "What's out that door?" And without waiting for an answer, he took off toward it.

When they'd pushed open the door, they were outside. Mr. Norris took a deep breath and studied the situation.

"Where are we going?" Addie asked, but got no answer.

"I think...no, that's not it, but...yes, of course, I know where we are," he said, taking off at a quick pace. "This is the terrace where the formal garden used to be. All gone for now....For crying out loud, be careful! Don't trip on the ridiculous horseshoe stakes they've put in. Or the croquet wickets...It's a regular minefield out here in the dark!"

They had come to the ivy-covered walls of the old original house. Addie had to hurry to keep up. Mr.

Norris ran one hand over the stone walls, pulling the ivy vines aside every few feet.

He muttered to himself.

"Somewhere along in here…Where…?" Then, "HA! I knew it!"

There was an old wooden door behind the ivy. With a heavy bolt and padlock locking it tight.

Mr. Norris, as usual, shook it long and hard anyway. After several colorful swear words, he finally gave up.

"Why don't I go look for a big rock," said Addie. "The padlock looks pretty rusty. Maybe we could smash it."

He nodded. Addie thought she saw a glint of hope in his eyes.

"I'll stay here," he said, "and see what I can do."

She went off, trying to remember if she'd seen any rocks. She'd only been gone a minute when she heard something. A bang? A screech of nails being yanked out of old wood? She wasn't sure, but she was back at the door in an instant, to find Mr. Norris doubled over. He waved her away.

"Just catching my breath. I need a moment."

While his breathing slowed and returned to normal, she looked behind him. The padlock and bolt were swinging on one limp nail and the door was open.

"How…?" was all she could say.

He cleared his throat. That deep, rumbling sound she remembered from the first time she met him.

"No questions," he rasped. He straightened up, his dark eyes on her. "And don't tell anyone. Come on, up we go."

A stairway inside went up and up and around and around.

Addie suddenly remembered.

"Is this the tower?"

"What do you think?" he said.

The stairs were difficult for him, and hardly any light came in through the small windows. Finally, they came to a door at the top. Addie dreaded the thought of another padlock, but there was none, and with a shove from both of them, the door scraped open.

"Ahh, we made it."

They were standing outside on the round, flat roof of the tower. There was a wall running around at waist height.

Mr. Norris stared out into the darkness and patted the wall gently.

"My father had this built. Of course, it didn't go at all with the rest of the house. My mother thought he was crazy, but he loved being up high and looking at the stars at night." He looked up. "This was my favorite place as a boy."

"Wow, it's really something," said Addie.

"Mmm. Once or twice I even slept up here. This and the pond on summer afternoons were my favorite places growing up."

They stood together in silence as memories came and went.

"My favorite place on summer afternoons was Granny Lu's garage," said Addie, leaning over the wall. "When it was really hot, we'd open up the big garage door, drag in some chairs, and sip ice tea through those bendy straws while we watched TV."

"Bendy straws?"

"Yeah, really. It was so fun. And sometimes the ice cream truck would come by." Addie looked up. Only one or two stars peeked out from the clouds. "In winter, my favorite place was Granny Lu's salon, which was in part of her house. Lulu's House of Hair. I'd hang out there after school. It was nice and warm from the hair dryer, her friends would be there, and we had a pink Christmas tree."

"Please tell me you didn't say pink?"

"Pink with silver tinsel! Granny Lu put presents for her clients under the tree, and sometimes they'd bring presents for me." Addie propped her elbows on the wall and rested her chin on her fists. "What about you? What was your favorite place in the winter?"

Mr. Norris took a moment to think.

"I guess it was the library—"

Addie interrupted. "You mean like the public library?"

"No," he said, frowning, "people used to have rooms in their houses they called the library. That's where we had a fire in the fireplace every evening, my mother and I, and it's where we had our tree at Christmas." He looked down at her. "It was green."

"Where was your father?"

"Are you always such a snoop?"

She waited.

"He was away a lot, doing scientific research for the government."

"Really? Weird, creepy stuff or boring, annoying stuff?"

He pointed a cane toward her.

"I don't talk about my private affairs."

"I know, I know," she said, looking away. "You don't talk about anything to anyone unless you're mad at them."

"That's rude!"

"Sorry."

"And unfair! I've been talking to you all evening!"

"I said I was sorry."

Addie wrapped her arms around her and shivered.

"We probably better go," she said.

Before she opened the door to the stairs, though, she said, "Thanks for sticking up for my mom with Mrs. Sloat."

Behind her, Mr. Norris said, "I didn't do it all for you, you know, or her. Made my day to needle that Sloat woman."

Going down the tower stairs was harder for him than going up. He tapped heavily with his canes and stepped carefully.

"Oh, well, with luck and a bit of exercise, I won't be here much longer," he said.

Addie didn't respond, but her heart speeded up. The question of how long she and Tish would also be there hung heavy in the air around her and in every breath she took.

CHAPTER 10

A few days later, Addie was showing Mr. Norris the dolls outside Miss Trotter's door while Tish went back to his old house to get some clothes he wanted.

Miss Trotter must have heard them and peeked around her door.

"Hi, Miss Trotter," said Addie. Mr. Norris started to bolt as if he'd been caught looking at something he shouldn't, but Addie grabbed his jacket.

"Whoa," she whispered to him, "that's not how you make friends here." She turned back. "Miss Trotter, this is Mr. Norris. I wanted him to see your dolls. You've moved them."

Miss Trotter and Mr. Norris both nodded without looking at each other. Miss Trotter bent down to straighten a little dress.

"I put them in some warmer clothes today...for the

cooler weather. How do you think their outfits look? Do you think they go together?"

Addie nodded while keeping a tight hold on Mr. Norris, who kept trying to slide away. "They are incredible. Wilma said you make all their clothes. You really do?"

Miss Trotter smiled and blushed.

The elevator at the end of the hall whirred to a stop, and before the door was fully open Minerva Swift beetled down the hall on her red scooter at full tilt.

"Watch out, everyone!" she called. "Babs Duckworthy is on the lookout for people to interview for the Happy Valley newsletter, and"—she zeroed in on Mr. Norris—"she's particularly after you!"

Mr. Norris turned pale. Miss Trotter vanished into her room, silently closing the door behind her. The elevator whirred to a stop again.

Minerva Swift looked from Addie to Mr. Norris.

"Into my room," she said briskly. With one last glance down the hall, she called to Mr. Greenberg, sitting as usual outside his room by the elevator, "Malcolm, don't give us away."

Addie could have sworn he winked.

"Addie, close the door," said Ms. Swift, once they were inside. "If she knocks, don't open it." Ms. Swift went around the room turning off her radio and putting a cloth over the birdcage to silence her parakeet.

"Sit down, Mr. Norris," she said.

He did as he was told.

"Who is this terrible woman?" he whispered.

Minerva sat down across from him.

"Babs Duckworthy lives in one of those 'Country Estate' townhomes, not far from the Barkers. She's in charge of the newsletter and takes her job very seriously. She is the world's worst snoop and will stop at nothing to pry information... let's be frank and call it gossip...out of anyone."

Addie thought she saw Mr. Norris shiver.

"Well, I will refuse to talk to her," he said.

Minerva Swift laughed.

"You can try, but she won't give up. She's in cahoots with Mrs. Sloat and Dr. Barker, and they love to know the gossip about residents. And you, unfortunately, being from the family who owned this whole property, are in their crosshairs."

Mr. Norris looked like he might be sick.

"Well, I don't want anyone looking into my private affairs!" He stood up and started to pace. "They can try, but I...I—"

Addie held her finger to her lips to shush him.

They could hear a woman's voice.

"GOOD AFTERNOON, MR. GREENBERG!"

Minerva Swift whispered, "She thinks he's deaf."

"HOW ARE YOU? HAVE YOU SEEN MR. NORRIS TODAY?"

Then they heard,

Knock, knock, knock. "Miss Trotter?" *Knock, knock, knock* on their door. "Ms. Swift?" *Knock, knock, knock.* "Mrs. Firillo?" *Knock, knock, knock.* "Mr. Trippling? Wilma, where is everybody today?"

Their voices drifted farther and farther away down the other hall.

"They'll be going to your room," said Minerva.

Mr. Norris breathed in with his eyes closed.

"Thank God I'm not there."

"You'd better stay here till she's gone. That is, if you want to."

"Thank you," he said. "I am extremely grateful."

"Me too," said Addie. "Tish and I don't want Mrs. Sloat to know I hang out here every day after school." She went to the covered birdcage. "Can I take a peek?"

"Just a peek," said Ms. Swift. "But come back another day and you can see him and hear him sing."

Mr. Norris went and stood in front of a wall of books.

"You've got quite a library here."

Minerva Swift gave a small laugh.

"This is only a remnant of what I used to have." She sighed. "I gave most of my books to the university where I taught."

She turned to Addie.

"Adelaide, do you like to read?"

"Well, not a lot."

"Oh, dear, don't say that." She got to her feet and went to the bookcase. "You like maps, though, don't you?" She moved her hands over the book spines. "I think I kept it...somewhere...ah, look here!" She pulled a book from the shelf and opened the cover. There was a map. "This was one of my favorite books growing up. *The Wind in the Willows.*"

Mr. Norris looked over their shoulders.

"Oh, I loved that book! Can I see it? I used to read it down by the pond. I imagined Ratty and Mole there...."

"I haven't read it in years," said Ms. Swift. "Adelaide! We will read it together. We can take as long as we want, but you must read it."

"Well...," said Addie, trying to think of an excuse.

"Mr. Norris, tell her she must read *The Wind in the Willows* with me."

"Yes, you should."

"Good, that's settled then," said Ms. Swift.

The two of them stood side by side like they were conspiring against her. Addie didn't want anyone telling her what to do, especially anyone telling her she had to read an old book. She stood in front of them, giving them her best scowl, as she realized they almost looked like two old friends.

"I've got to go," she said.

"I should be going also," said Mr. Norris. "Thank you again for rescuing us."

"Anytime," said Ms. Swift.

Addie opened the door carefully. The hall was empty except for good old Mr. Greenberg. She and Mr. Norris slipped out.

They'd made it halfway across the lounge when an imposing woman sprang out of the dining room, where Mrs. A, B, C, and D were playing cards.

"Mr. Norris, I've found you at last!"

CHAPTER
11

Addie left school the next day with her friends Ivy and Janelle, who were also walkers. It wasn't always easy making new friends, but she'd had a fair amount of practice at the different schools she'd gone to. And besides, she thought, if she could teach Dickson and Mr. Norris how to make friends, then she should be able to do it herself.

"Call me if you can't do the math problems," said Ivy, waving. Addie thanked her lucky stars one of her new friends was a math whiz. She waved to Janelle and started to look for Dickson. She was in such a good mood that, for the first time ever, she couldn't wait to see him.

Finally, he came, dragging his backpack beside him. But as they walked and she told him what Tish had seen at Mr. Norris's house, he got bouncier and bouncier until he looked like he was on a trampoline.

"NO...WAY!" he said over and over, holding on to his glasses.

"I'm not kidding! Tish was looking for the socks and pajamas he wanted. She looked where he told her. But then, in the very bottom of the very last box in the closet, there was this big silver belt and black boots and a blue stretchy one-piece suit that had silver streamers on the back. And she right away thought of the WWE shows you watch on TV."

Dickson was shaking his head back and forth.

"Wow!" he breathed. "And did the belt have *World Wrestling Entertainment* on it?"

"All Tish saw was a big *B.*"

"*B?* That doesn't make sense. The official title belts have *WWE* on them." Dickson was thinking hard. "Maybe it's not his...but whose is it? Maybe just a costume?"

"Can you really picture Mr. Norris at a costume party? Because I can't!" said Addie. "You know, Brad said he wondered what Mr. Norris used to do, because he still has strong muscles and moves like an athlete. And the other night, there was a door he opened somehow...."

Dickson was looking at her. Then he studied the ground.

"We have to investigate!" he said.

With that, he took off.

After checking in with Wilma and Tish and saying they'd be "right outside," they crossed two parking lots for staff, passed an entrance to the nursing home wing, and crossed another road to the new HVV townhomes, before coming to a small gravel drive leading to the farmhouse and garage.

The two buildings were built next to each other on

two sides of a square courtyard. The farmhouse was a simple white house with a porch. The garage was also white, with three big double doors on the ground floor. An outdoor stairway went up at one end of it to an apartment above.

They tried the front and back doors of the farmhouse. Both were locked. Through the windows, which were also locked, they could see a kitchen, living room, dining room, and study.

"We want to get upstairs to the bedroom," said Dickson, looking up.

They walked around the house three times. There was no tree to climb, no basement door to check. They considered climbing the gutter pipe, but it was so flimsy it practically came away in Addie's hands when she tried it.

"Let's check the garage," she said.

Each of the three massive wooden doors had a hefty bolt and padlock. The only windows were high up and covered with paper on the inside.

They went up the stairway on the far side of the garage. The door had a window, but all they could see was some kind of small apartment that looked like it hadn't been used in years.

Dickson sighed as they went down the stairs again.

"Rats."

"Let's look around the house again in case he hid a key outside," said Addie.

They split up, checking behind shutters, under rocks and leaves, and under doormats.

Addie was behind the house, trying again to push open windows, when she heard loud voices out front. She peeked around the corner of the house.

"Oh no, not another one!" Mr. Norris shouted on seeing her. He steadied himself with one cane and pointed the other one toward her. Dickson was in front of him and had suddenly shrunk several sizes. Tish was holding on to Mr. Norris to steady him while he tried to shake her off.

"What do you two think you're doing here?" he yelled. "And don't give me some story." His eyes blazed at Dickson. "Trying the door and windows. The law calls that breaking and entering. I'll call the police! I'll tell your mothers!" He remembered Tish was beside him. "Do you see what your daughter is up to? I am going to tell the Sloat about this!"

They were caught off guard by a wail that was growing and swelling. Dickson had sunk to the ground, letting loose a series of ever-louder soggy cries.

"No—o—o...you can't tell my m—m—mother!"

The three of them looked at him.

Mr. Norris humphed.

"It's called consequences, young man."

Tish went over and knelt down beside Dickson.

"I'm sure we can explain it to your mom. I'll talk to her. Who is she, by the way?"

It took a minute between wet snuffles to get the words out.

Tish stood up.

"Who did you say?"

Dickson spoke up. Then they all heard.

"Mrs. S—Sloat...is my mother."

Addie, Tish, and Mr. Norris looked back and forth at one another.

"No way, Dickson," breathed Addie.

"Stand up, you little delinquent!" Mr. Norris snapped. Dickson stood up.

Mr. Norris contemplated him for a minute.

"You have my deepest sympathies," he said gruffly. "Here, take this." He handed Dickson a large linen handkerchief.

After Dickson blew out several cupfuls of snot and tears, fogging up his glasses, he looked up at Mr. Norris with bleary eyes.

"We wanted to know if you'd been in the WWE," he said weakly. "You know, the big silver belt and the blue suit thing...."

Mr. Norris peered down at him, looking confused.

"The silver belt...?" Mr. Norris's eyes pivoted slowly to Tish. "What did you..." His voice deepened to a level between a whisper and a low roar.

Tish hesitated, took a deep breath, and said, "I was looking for the clothes you wanted and I came across a silver belt and the rest...and..." She looked at Addie and Dickson. "I know how much Dickson loves the wrestling stuff, and—"

Mr. Norris turned away from them and swore.

"First that Babs Duckworthy woman and now you three! Prying, snooping, asking questions. My past is private! Why can't anyone understand that?"

"Sorry, Mr. Norris...really," said Dickson in a small voice, "and I won't ask any more questions, only..." Dickson was on fire with curiosity.

Addie thought, *Uh-oh, here we go.* You had to hand it to Dickson for being persistent.

"Could you teach me one of your signature moves?"

"My signature moves?" said Mr. Norris, looking confused.

"Yeah! So I can take down those kids at school!" Dickson did his best punch and kick. "They won't know what hit them. I'll be the New Avenging Dickson Sloat the Third!"

CHAPTER 12

Later that night, Addie sat in the deserted lounge of Arborvine with a page of math problems on her lap. She'd already called Ivy for help, but she still had a bunch to do. The tail end of a storm was blowing outside, spraying raindrops and leaves against the glass of the terrace door. If Uncle Tim couldn't pick them up later, she and Tish were going to have a wet bus ride home. They'd probably miss the kids' bedtime, but maybe it was just as well. The last time they'd come home right at bedtime, Bella and Logan had gotten so excited it took an extra hour to settle them down, and Aunt Tina, who had an exam in one of her accounting courses the next day, had not been happy.

Those memories made the peace and quiet of Arborvine even better, especially after the earlier adventure at Mr. Norris's house. Addie had been afraid he would complain about it to someone at HVV, and afraid the blame would then land on Tish. But Mr. Norris was so bothered about Mrs. Sloat being Dickson's mother that he'd promised not to say a word as long as they wouldn't go snooping again. So, for the moment, Tish's job was okay, Mrs. Sloat still thought Dickson went to business camp every day after school, and Dickson was crazy happy, hoping for the inside scoop on WWE moves.

Giving up on her math, Addie went down the hall to Mrs. Barker's room to see if she could get a dollar from Tish for the drink machine.

Tish had been asked to stay late again to help Mrs. Barker until she was ready for bed. Mr. Norris was getting better and needed her less, so Tish was being assigned to other residents.

"I'm worried about Genevieve," Tish had said while they ate dinner in the cafeteria earlier. "I think she's gone downhill since she's been at Arborvine. They keep changing her meds, but all that seems to do is make her fuzzier and weaker."

Tish was helping Mrs. Barker pick out clothes to wear the next day as Addie left the room with a dollar. She was going past Mr. Norris's room next door when she heard a squealing, wrenching sound, along with a strangled growl.

Addie checked up and down the hall. Being right outside his partly open door, it seemed she was the only person to hear it.

She peeked into his room just in time to see the last bit of him going out the window.

"Oh, for heaven's sake!" Granny Lu would have said. "Now what!"

If she didn't catch up to him, he'd be gone in the dark. There was no time to get anyone. Addie closed his door softly behind her. She grabbed a blanket off the bed to wrap herself in, sat on the windowsill, swiveled her legs over it to the outside, and pulled the squeaking window closed behind her.

There was more wind than rain, but it was still a nasty night. A night no one but a crazy old man picking his way along with two canes would want to be out in.

At first, she couldn't see him anywhere. Only in the parking lot lights was she able at last to spot his dark, lumbering shape.

When she caught up to him, she grabbed his jacket and shouted over the wind.

"What are you doing!"

He was so startled, she had to hold him to steady him.

"Let go of me! There's something I have to do. Go away!" He turned and headed into the wind like a determined force of nature, even with Addie trying to pull him back.

"Why can't you do it tomorrow? Tish can help you tomorrow."

"Go back inside," he growled.

"But...Mrs. Sloat will find a way to blame Tish if anything happens. Please, come back!" Addie cried, doing her best to hold on.

He stopped under a big oak tree where they were a bit out of the rain, and he leaned against the trunk.

"Listen to me," he said, shaking free of her grip, "this is something that doesn't concern you. But it's important, it's something I have to...Are you wearing my blanket? You look like a street urchin straight out of Dickens."

"Whatever," she said. "Are you going to your house? Is that what this is about? The WWE stuff...the blue suit and the silver belt?"

He closed his eyes, and a growl began deep in his chest and rose like the roar of the wind itself.

"I don't want them!" he cried. "I never did!" He looked wild and angry. "I don't know why I've kept them this long, but no one else is ever going to find them."

He gathered himself together to head off again.

"Wait!" she said. "Wait and do it tomorrow." This time she got a grip on his jacket with one hand and his cane with the other and wasn't going to let go.

"Trust me, wait till tomorrow," she said. "If you get rid of your important things, you're going to regret it. Think about it."

He tried to shrug her off and went out into the rain again, dragging her with him.

"Listen, you old geezer, you're going to be sorry. I know it!" She was holding on to him with one hand and hitting his arm with the other to make him stop. "I don't have anything anymore!" She was shouting to him over the wind, but he kept plowing ahead. "Every time we moved, we left more behind. Everything's gone, Granny

Lu is gone! I have nothing to remember her with. My book of maps, that's it!"

She didn't know if he'd heard her. She didn't know what else to do, so she kicked him. Hard.

"Ow!" He stopped.

"Do you hear me?" She stood there looking up at him with raindrops and tears dissolving together down her cheeks. "Only maps! Nothing of Granny Lu's to remember, no Dream Box where we put the coins and stamps she bought, our lottery tickets, postcards from clients, tinsel, bendy straws. No pictures, no special anything. So don't go getting rid of those things. I'm telling you. Don't!"

Mr. Norris glittered with anger as he looked down at her.

"You!" he bellowed. "You drive me crazy!" He huffed and puffed, but he took it down a notch. "What if I agreed to wait till tomorrow? Would that stop your... hysterics?"

"I am not...!" Addie didn't finish but grabbed his sleeve and dragged him back toward Arborvine. "Come on!"

They were crossing one of the driveways when a car's headlights suddenly came up the hill at them. With the wind, it was impossible to hear cars coming. It was also impossible to move quickly with Mr. Norris in tow.

In an instant the car's headlights shattered their world into a flash of white, a blare of horn; the wind roared, and then... and then... Addie found herself holding on to Mr. Norris on the other side of the road as the car's red taillights disappeared in the dark. At first, she thought the car must have hit them, because she'd felt air and rain rushing past her face and she was off the ground, thrown through the air, or... She didn't know what had happened, only when something happens that fast, you can never really understand it. She felt fuzzy, as if she couldn't remember everything that had happened. But they were okay, they weren't hurt. She stood there, becoming aware of the heavy blanket reeking of wet wool, her squelching shoes, and the sleeve of Mr. Norris's tweed jacket that she held tight in her fist.

He gave her a nudge.

"Let's go," he growled, low and out of breath. "That's enough excitement for one night."

CHAPTER 13

Later that night, while Addie and Tish lay on the inflatable bed they shared in Bella's room, Addie told Tish part of what had happened. The parts that made sense.

"I'll get them to look at his window first thing tomorrow," Tish said. "Maybe they can nail it shut! And don't worry, I'll keep an eye on him. Gee, if he doesn't want the old costume, he could at least give it to Dickson. Wouldn't he love it?" Tish swore. "Move those feet of yours, they're like ice cubes!"

It took Addie a long time to warm up, and then she fell into dreams that came and went through the night. Sometimes she was floating, sometimes she was flying. There were blinding flashes of light, sometimes only stars, but there was always the rush and blow of wind.

☼

The next day, Addie and Dickson had a third person on their walk to HVV. Marwa was a new fifth grader whose mother had gotten a job there in housekeeping.

When the school principal learned that Marwa would also be walking to HVV, she placed Marwa in Addie's class, asked Addie to help her settle in to school and show her the way to HVV.

Addie knew a thing or two about being new at a school so it wasn't a big deal to show Marwa the ropes, though at first she didn't think they'd have much in common.

For one thing, it was obvious Marwa had fashion sense. She walked in on her first day, shy and quiet, the beginning of a smile, wearing a black top under a bright pink jacket, a black-and-white polka-dot skirt, black leggings, and black sneakers. She wore a headband with a large white flower on one side.

Marwa's family had recently come from Iraq and she was still learning English but, as Addie learned, not knowing the words didn't slow Marwa down one bit.

"I LOVE it!" was Marwa's favorite expression. And she really did seem to love everything and everyone she met, even the mound of tuna salad dumped on her lunch tray.

"Tuna? What is tuna?" she asked, eyes fixed on the round gray scoop. But after one taste, and seeing everyone else eating it, she was sold.

"I LOVE it!"

Marwa said, or tried to say, whatever she wanted, no holding back. She was just about the most enthusiastic person Addie had ever met and it seemed to rub off on everyone around her.

"My mom is really, really happy to get the job. She couldn't work when we first come from Iraq, but now she has the paper that say she can work. She was teacher, but she loves to clean, so she is happy! So, where we going?"

"We go this way, Marwa," said Addie as they walked outside after school. She had never seen anyone so happy after their first day at a new school. It made her laugh.

"We'll wait here a minute for Dickson, the other kid I told you about, then we'll walk over to HVV. Do you know where your mother is working? We can go try and find her when we get there. Between me and Dickson, I think we know most of the place."

"Mmm." Marwa shook her head. "I don't know where. Maybe we can ask."

Dickson appeared and, after an introduction, they started on their way, Marwa practically skipping and Dickson droning on with his introduction to Happy Valley Village. It felt to Addie like it had only been a few days since he'd been telling her the same things. Or maybe a few years. Sometimes, it seemed time had a way of stretching and shrinking like a rubber band.

However, she had one important bit of information to add to Dickson's lecture.

"If you hear anything about Mrs. Sloat...she's in charge of the whole place, and she's...well, she's Dickson's mother. Just so you know."

Dickson was poking under leaves.

"And she can't know I come over right after school," he added, straightening up. "Okay, Marwa?"

"So if she's around," said Addie, "Dickson has to hide. And we do too, because she doesn't want kids around all the time."

Marwa's eyes had gotten big and round.

"Okay," she said, looking from one to the other.

When they got to HVV, Wilma gave them the good news. Mrs. Sloat would be away all afternoon at a meeting.

"Yessss!" cried Dickson, making a victory fist. "Marwa, this is your lucky day! We can give you the grand tour."

Which was exactly what they did.

First they found Marwa's mother where she was doing a load of sheets in one of the laundry rooms. Mrs. Omar, in a pretty flowered headscarf, had the same dark, smiling eyes as her daughter. She was overjoyed to see Marwa, wrapped her in a big hug, while saying hello to Addie and Dickson. She and Marwa talked in Arabic, Marwa bouncing and laughing.

"My mom wants to know about my first day of school. And she wants to know if she can meet me at the big main door at 5 o'clock?" said Marwa.

"Sure," said Addie. "We'll get you there."

Marwa smiled and said something in Arabic to her mother.

Her mother nodded and patted Addie's cheek.

"I told her you take care of me," said Marwa to Addie. Addie laughed and shook her head, but Marwa was serious. "Really. You do! You know everything, Addie!"

"Hey guys," said Dickson, "can we do the rest of the tour now?"

Back on Arborvine, Marwa fell in love with Miss Trotter's dolls. The dolls wore coats and hats now. The lion had a striped scarf and the monkey wore crocheted earmuffs that covered his missing ear. Miss Trotter was refilling the candy dish with Halloween candy when they came by.

"I LOVE her!" Marwa whispered to Addie.

"Malcolm was the one who suggested that color green for the monkey's earmuffs. I think he was right, don't you agree?" whispered Miss Trotter.

Addie looked over at Mr. Greenberg in his wheelchair. "Does he talk to you?"

"Oh, yes. Well, that is, when he feels like it. He was an artist, you know, before his stroke. He has a wonderful color sense." She looked at her next-door neighbor shyly. "Don't you, Malcolm?"

There wasn't much he could do in the neck brace, but Addie noticed a couple of fingers wiggling.

They introduced Marwa to Mrs. A, B, C, and D, playing cards in the dining room. The ladies were intrigued by the news Marwa was from Iraq and wanted to know about her family. They made Marwa promise to tell them more when they weren't deep in a bridge game.

Minerva Swift and her scooter weren't at home, but Mrs. Firillo and Mr. Trippling definitely were. Their argument and Izzy's barks spilled out into the hallway.

"Patsy, you said we were going to work on Italian lesson number four today, don't you remember? Where's your calendar? I wrote it down for you."

"Oh, for heaven's sakes, Gene, who checks their calendar all the time? I promised the garden club I'd meet them in the library, and I have to take Izzy out before I do that. Let's do Italian tomorrow."

"But you've said that for the past three days! Really, Patsy, I'm going to start leaving you notes on your door every morning. You need a social director!"

Mr. Trippling came stomping out of Mrs. Firillo's room, batting the vines aside, with Mrs. Firillo close behind him.

"There's no need—" she said, but stopped short when she saw them. "Oh my goodness! Why, it's...Gene, look who's here!"

Holding Izzy, Mrs. Firillo leaned down to Marwa.

"Oh, dearie, did you say you were coming to visit today?" She spoke in her softest voice. "I completely forgot! And what a wonderful flower!"

Marwa had big question marks in her eyes as she turned to Addie.

Gene put a hand gently on Mrs. Firillo's arm.

"Addie, Dickson, you've brought someone new with you," he said. "An introduction?"

"This is Marwa," said Addie. "Her mother's started working here."

There was silence from Mrs. Firillo.

"Marwa," repeated Mr. Trippling. "Nice to meet you." He turned to Mrs. Firillo. "You thought she looked familiar, didn't you?" He spoke gently. "She does kind of look like one of your granddaughters. Where's that picture of her? Can I see it again?"

With a wink over his shoulder to them, he escorted Mrs. Firillo back into her room.

"Okayyyy," breathed Marwa.

"I need to use Mr. Trippling's computer," said Dickson, "but let's finish the tour of the other hallway first."

They passed the rooms for Mrs. A, B, C, and D, then Mr. Norris's room, but Wilma had said he was at the gym.

"Can't you tell how nice and quiet it is?"

Addie hoped Brad was keeping a close eye on him and that he hadn't escaped back to his house during the day.

At Mrs. Barker's room next door, Addie gave a little knock and opened the door wider.

"Tish?"

Her mother was reading to Mrs. Barker, who was lying down on her bed. Tish waved to Addie to come in.

"Hey, this is Marwa," Addie whispered. "Her mom's working in housekeeping." Mrs. Barker's eyes fluttered open. "Hi, Mrs. Barker. This is Marwa."

The old lady waved her hand to them.

Tish whispered to Addie. "Genevieve's been all worked up. She's lost her pearls, and we can't find them anywhere."

Addie whispered back to her, "Hey, has Mr. Norris been here all day?"

"Yup, we've had our eyes glued to him!"

Back in the hall, Dickson led the way.

"Addie, you can keep showing Marwa around, okay?

I want to ask Mr. Trippling if I can use his computer."
He lowered his voice. "Marwa, we think we have a real
CELEBRITY here at HVV!"

The way Marwa's eyes opened wide showed she obviously knew the word.

"A celebrity?"

Dickson nodded with a wide grin to Addie.

"We have to tell her, right?"

Addie didn't know what to say.

"You know, Mr. Norris really, really cares about his
privacy," she said to Dickson.

"Yeah, but come on, the WWE is all about the public and putting on a show! How can it be private? That's
what I've got to research online. If I post about his costume and the B on the belt, someone must know who he
used to be."

Marwa's head went back and forth.

"Who...what is...WWE?" she said.

Dickson couldn't keep it in a second longer.

"You can't tell anyone, Marwa. Promise! Okay, so..."
And he went into the details of Tish finding the silver
belt and how Brad said Mr. Norris must have been some
kind of athlete and the blue suit, the silver streamers...
until he stopped to breathe.

He'd been talking so fast, Addie was watching Marwa
to see if she was understanding. Marwa looked confused
at first, and then it was like a spotlight went on. Her eyes
got bigger and bigger.

"I know, I know!" she cried when Dickson stopped

to get a breath. "I know who you are saying." Her eyes filled with tears.

"I have been looking ever since we come to America. You know, when we first come?" she whispered. "I saw one."

Addie and Dickson looked at each other.

"We are in New York City," said Marwa, "in big, big Times Square, and I get lost. And what do you think, but Superman, he comes and saves me! He takes me to a policeman who finds my parents. I was so happy! Everyone knows, of course, that superheroes live in America, and now I have met one! But after that? No," she said, dropping her head and looking sad. "No more." She lit up with a smile that practically sparkled. "Until now!"

"No, Marwa," Addie said, shaking her head. "Not a superhero, really, not a superhero."

But the more she and Dickson tried to explain, the more Marwa's eyes shone.

CHAPTER 14

It was the next afternoon and Marwa had still not met Mr. Norris. As soon as they got to HVV, they asked where he was, only to find out he'd been driven to an appointment at his bank in town. Tish had gone with him to help.

Marwa was crushed.

"Next-best thing!" said Dickson, knocking on Mr. Trippling's door. "Let's see if there are any replies to my posts from yesterday."

As Addie, Dickson, and Marwa sat in front of his computer, Mr. Trippling hovered behind them.

"You aren't doing anything you shouldn't be doing, are you?" he said, wiping his glasses. "No video games, right?"

"It's okay, Mr. Trippling," said Dickson. "We're doing research...for school." He hunched closer to the screen. "Have you been having problems with your computer today? It's so slow. I think I'd better run a virus scan."

Mr. Trippling leaned closer over their heads.

"Oh, no, don't tell me it's caught one of those germ things! Oh, dear," he said, breathing deeply. "Dickson, see if you can fix it. I think I'll just lie down for a minute." He sank onto his bed across the room.

Marwa had already gone out into the hall when she saw Mrs. Firillo pass by with Izzy. The three of them were going outside for a walk when Addie went to get her backpack in the lounge.

Addie had promised Minerva Swift she would read with her. She wasn't looking forward to it. She dragged her backpack down the hall and, just before knocking on the door, decided she needed another candy from Miss Trotter's dish.

She took one, opened it, then took another. She went and stood in front of Mr. Greenberg. He was sitting in his wheelchair in his usual spot next door.

She held the candy up in front of him.

"Hey, Mr. Greenberg. Want one?"

His eyes did an ever-so-slow turn to her.

His fingers on one hand did their wiggly thing again.

Addie smiled, opened the candy wrapper, and dropped it in his hand.

"It's a lemon one. Is lemon okay?"

He managed a thumbs-up.

She watched him maneuver the candy to his mouth.

"Wow, good job, Mr. Greenberg!" She gave him a double thumbs-up.

As she knocked on Minerva Swift's door, the parakeet added to Ms. Swift's "Come in" with its own flourish of chirps and squawks.

Ms. Swift tried to shush it. "Oh, be quiet, Hermes."

They settled in on the couch with *The Wind in the Willows*. It helped that it had a map. Ms. Swift showed Addie all the places that would be in the story. They looked at it a long time. Then Ms. Swift asked about Addie's maps, so Addie told her about the maps she'd made of Granny Lu's and the places they'd lived since.

"You've had lots of adventures for someone your age," said Ms. Swift quietly, "maybe not all bad, but not all good either. You know, I think that's why I came to love books so much. When I was young, I wasn't very happy. My parents were older and very strict. They didn't have much time for me, but I found I could always go somewhere else, somewhere wonderful, between the covers of a book. And one of my very favorite places was the world of the river in this book."

Ms. Swift started to read, and the story was, as she said, someplace wonderful. The Rat and Mole rowing on the river, meeting Otter and crazy Mr. Toad, having a lazy picnic on the riverbank. Every few pages she stopped and made Addie read a part, which was not a whole lot of fun, but the story kept Addie going.

The phone rang and Ms. Swift went to answer it. While she talked, Addie's thoughts wandered.

When Ms. Swift came back, Addie said, "Ms. Swift,

do you think people can do things...like, unusual things?"

"Please call me Minerva. I'm much more of a Minerva than a Ms. Swift. What do you mean by unusual?"

"I don't know. It sounds weird, but what if you thought you were going to be run over by a car and suddenly it's gone by and you're safe on the other side of the road and you're not sure how you got there?"

Minerva thought a minute.

"Are you thinking you might have unusual abilities?"

Addie let out a laugh. "Oh, no, not me! It was Mr.—it was someone I was with."

Minerva turned a ring around and around on her finger.

"And could this person be Mr. Norris?"

Addie looked down at her lap.

"Do you think he's weird?" she said. "Has he ever looked at you with eyes that look like they go right through you? And one night...I think he might be really strong...."

Minerva looked closely at her.

"Excuse me for asking," she said, "but he hasn't done or said anything inappropriate, has he?"

"Oh, no, nothing like that. He's just...different." Addie laughed. "We think he used to be a wrestler. You know, one of those guys who wears a costume and wrestles on TV? But Marwa thinks he's a superhero, and we can't talk her out of it!"

Minerva burst into a laugh. "Well, that's a good one! Wrestling is funny enough, but Mr. Norris a superhero!"

She chuckled. Then her smile left. She got up and went to her bureau. "Let me show you something over here."

Addie went and stood next to her.

"See these things? Here's my weekly pill organizer, here are my hearing aid batteries, these are reminder cards for doctors' appointments. This is what 'old' looks like, Adelaide. It happens differently for everyone. I'm sure it's different for me than it is for Mr. Norris and than it was for your Granny Lu. What I'm trying to say is that maybe Mr. Norris is losing some of his faculties," she said, tapping the side of her head. "Losing some of his abilities, and maybe it looks like special powers to you. Could that be it?"

"I don't know, but I don't think that's it. He seems plenty sharp to me. He's only here because he was falling."

Minerva nodded.

"Well, why don't you ask your mother? Maybe she's noticed something."

Addie saw a small photograph on the bureau in a silver frame that was so tarnished it was almost black. "Who's that?" she said, pointing.

Minerva picked it up.

"That's my niece with her husband and daughter. She's probably about your age now."

"Do you see them?"

Minerva pinched her lips together.

"Not much. They're busy, and we don't communicate a lot." She sighed. "I know that doesn't sound very nice, but at least they won't miss me much when I'm gone."

"Well, you should invite them over," said Addie.

The awkward silence was broken by a sudden mini-commotion outside the door, then a quick knock, and Dickson burst through the doorway with Marwa right behind.

"I got a reply, several actually. Come see, Addie!"

Addie remembered to thank Minerva and said yes, she would come to read the next day, before hurrying with the others to Mr. Trippling's computer.

"Look!" said Dickson, pointing to the screen.

Marwa nudged him, putting a finger to her lips and pointing to Mr. Trippling, who lay flat on his bed with a silk scarf over his eyes.

On the site where Dickson had posted questions, there were a bunch of replies. Some said they had never heard of such an outfit in WWE; others had a few ideas, a few questions.

One reply, however, said they had heard of just such an outfit and said they knew something about the letter *B*. They asked for more information, such as where the outfit was found and who owned it. They said they'd been interested in the history of WWE for a long time and would be happy to help.

CHAPTER 15

"I have some sad news," said Tish as she met the three of them a few days later at the back door. "Mrs. B died this morning." She looked at Dickson. "Your mother's been around more than usual, so let's go downstairs." She led the way down to the basement. "Someone phoned from the HVV hair salon this morning to say that Mrs. B had been under the hair dryer a long time and wasn't responding." Tish shook her head and smiled sadly at Addie. "Under a hair dryer... What would Granny Lu have thought about that?"

"Mrs. B was nice," said Dickson.

"Yeah," said Marwa.

"It'll be different without her," said Addie. "She was always around."

Tish squeezed her tight and kissed the top of her head.

"It's hard when somebody goes. We'll miss her," Tish murmured into Addie's hair.

Addie scrunched up into one corner of the sofa. She kept hearing Tish's words, "when somebody goes." The dark, quiet basement was nothing like when Granny Lu was going. Her house was filled with people wandering in and out, bringing food, discussing somewhere over Addie's head things that needed to be done. The hospital was the same. People talking in low voices, holding damp tissues, never sitting still for more than a minute.

Tish gave Addie a long look, then made sure they were settled in the storage compartment.

"Will you be okay hanging out here for a bit, guys? Dickson, are there snacks in there?"

He dug through the container.

"Yeah, Des left plenty. But there's nothing to drink."

"I'll bring more. And can I bring Mrs. B's cat? It's in a carrier but it's been howling and driving us all crazy."

Marwa's eyes lit up.

"I'll take care of the kitty!"

"You're a lifesaver, Marwa! I'll be back in a minute."

Tish reappeared shortly with juice and a carrier full of noisy cat.

Marwa tried everything, singing, soothing, waving, and pushing chips through the cage door. Nothing worked. Fluffy (the name on the carrier) huddled at the back, eyes half shut in slits. She made her emotional state clear by groaning, with an occasional hiss or yowl.

"Who's going to take care of Fluffy now?" said Marwa.

"Well, I can't because I'm allergic," said Dickson. He crumpled up a bag of cookies and sighed. "I hope we can go upstairs soon and get to Mr. Trippling's computer. I checked last night at home when Mom was busy and there was a reply from this one guy—"

"You know, I was thinking," said Addie, interrupting. "What if Mr. Norris is just crazy?" The others looked at her. "I mean, come on, it's possible."

She and Tish had talked about Mr. Norris a lot over the last few days. Tish admitted he was different, definitely, and odd, absolutely, but in the end, she thought everything weird could be explained by him being old. Your average old-guy loopiness.

Dickson wasn't going for it.

"No way! This person online says they've heard of a WWE outfit like this and they've heard of a wrestler with a *B*. They said they've been writing a history of WWE. They had lots of questions. Do you think Mr. Norris would ever be okay with somebody coming to interview him?"

"Now you're dreaming!" said Addie.

"I don't understand," said Marwa, wiggling a finger at Fluffy. "Why would a superhero stay hiding away? A superhero needs to be out everywhere, helping people, fighting bad guys, making movies."

"Marwa, he's not a superhero," said Dickson.

"And he's not doing any superhero things," said Addie. She turned to Dickson. "What if he's not anything?"

It was common sense, of course. A weird old man was

just that, nothing more. But then, how had he and Addie avoided being hit by the car?

With a hiss, Fluffy swiped a claw at the finger Marwa was poking through the wire.

"Ow!" cried Marwa. "Not nice, kitty!"

Suddenly, Addie wanted to get out of there. "I'm going to take Fluffy up and see if she'll eat something. Maybe she's hungry."

Addie lifted the hissing cat carrier.

"Let us know if it's quiet upstairs and we can come up," said Dickson.

It was anything but quiet in Arborvine.

There was a cluster of what looked like family members outside Mrs. B's room. Babs Duckworthy, with pad and pencil, was asking them about Mrs. B for an article she was writing for the newsletter.

Addie snuck past them into the kitchenette without a yowl from Fluffy. She was pouring some milk into a bowl when she heard a cry from Babs Duckworthy close by.

"There you are, Mr. Norris! I was hoping to catch you."

"Pardon me, can't stop," he grumbled.

But Babs did not defeat easily.

"I would love to try a 'Two Truths and a Lie' article for you. You know, you tell me three things and readers have to guess which two are true and which one is false?"

Mr. Norris caught sight of Addie and detoured into the kitchenette.

"Get this woman away from me!" he whispered, wild-eyed.

Addie picked Fluffy up, wrangling her tight in her arms before the cat had a chance to protest, and grabbed the bowl of milk.

"Sorry, Mrs. Duckworthy, Mr. Norris promised to help me with the cat," Addie muttered. "We think she might have…fleas."

Mrs. Duckworthy scooted back two feet.

"But we can't have fleas here!" she cried. "Do you really like cats, Mr. Norris? I can't stand them. I'm a dog person, myself…."

Her voice grew fainter and fainter as Addie and Mr. Norris hurried down the hall. When they made it to Mr. Norris's room, he closed the door sharply.

"I think we've lost her," he whispered, listening. "That cat doesn't really have fleas, does it?"

Addie put Fluffy down. She managed to growl and drink milk at the same time, then slipped under the bed.

"Nah, but I figured it sure would keep someone like Mrs. Duckworthy away."

"And where did the cat come from?"

After Addie explained, Mr. Norris said, "Well, it can't stay here."

"Okay," said Addie with a shrug. "Whatever, but I can't take it because Aunt Tina would never let us keep it at her house, and I'm telling you a cat with fleas would be like one of those invisible fences for Babs Duckworthy."

She could tell Mr. Norris was torn.

There were voices in the hall, but it wasn't Babs Duckworthy this time. Addie and Mr. Norris looked at each other. It was Mrs. Sloat and Dr. Barker. And Tish.

There was a murmur of voices as they went into Genevieve Barker's room next door. Wilma was called in. They heard her say she'd have an aide take Genevieve for a short walk in her wheelchair.

Dim sounds of voices floated through the wall, but soon the voices got so loud and sharp it was easy to hear what was going on.

"You have been Mrs. Barker's main companion," said Mrs. Sloat.

"Which isn't to say...," said Dr. Barker, "but we think if anyone had seen the pearls it would have been you."

"We've all been looking for them. Housekeeping looked through every one of her sheets when they changed the bed," Tish said.

"It's just that she wore them every day," said Dr. Barker. "She's more forgetful now, I admit, but she never took them off and then, when she did, she would always put them with her other jewelry. Right here in this dish."

"Believe me, I've looked every day since they went missing."

"So the question is, what are we going to do? In the meantime, please remember you were hired temporarily for a month...to see how things go. The month is half over, and now this," said Mrs. Sloat.

From her clipped voice, Addie could practically see her picture-perfect blond head riveted on Tish.

"Well, I—"

"What I mean is," interrupted Mrs. Sloat, "pearls don't just disappear. And if you don't know what happened, well then, who does?"

Addie could feel the temperature of the room next door shooting up.

"Look," said Tish, her voice rising, "I can stand here and tell you two a million times I don't know anything about the pearls and haven't seen them. But it's going to be a big waste of my time and yours. Go ahead and fire me if you want. I think you'd like to find any excuse. Right now, I'm overdue for a break. In case you didn't know, I work really hard at this job. But I'm going to go on break, and you two can let me know what you decide."

Addie could feel Mr. Norris watching her, but she refused to look at him. She waited till she heard Mrs. Sloat and Dr. Barker leave and then walked out of Mr. Norris's room, closing the door behind her.

She was partway down the hall when she heard Mr. Norris's call.

"What about the cat?"

At that moment, she really didn't care.

CHAPTER 16

Three days later, coming down the path in the woods, Addie saw them before they saw her. Tish and Mr. Norris were walking on the far side of the pond. It had been a prickly few days with Tish angry at everyone and everything, but now, the October sun had warmed the afternoon so that it felt almost like spring. It even sounded like spring with Aunt Tina's brother Matt criss-crossing the hill on the big lawnmower. Marwa was humming the latest pop song stuck in her head, while Dickson was back to finding bugs. Addie didn't mind waiting for him. It felt good to be in a thin jacket, standing still with her eyes closed, smelling the earth, listening to the birds.

"Addie!" Marwa squealed, grabbing her sleeve and shaking her. "It's Mr. Norris!" She took off at a run.

"Oh, boy," said Dickson, standing up. "We'd better go get her."

In the end, Tish had kept her job. But only just. She was talking about moving again, and when she was really in a mood, she'd pull up her sleeves to show her tattoos and threaten to find new places to get pierced. The pearls still hadn't been found, but there was no proof Tish was the thief. In fact, the Arborvine residents had only good things to say about her.

One surprise was that Mr. Norris had written a letter to Mrs. Sloat standing up for Tish. Addie suspected he'd done it partly to annoy Mrs. Sloat, but whatever the reason, it hadn't hurt. Of course, Mr. Norris also had a deal in mind when he told her about the letter. It was the cat.

"As soon as you find a home for that cat, out it goes," he said. "I'm only letting you leave it here because I never see it and it's my Babs Duckworthy defense. Until then, here's the deal...you have to clean the kitty litter every day. Why I let you put it in my closet I don't know. I may die from the fumes. I will pay for the food and litter, but you clean. Got it?"

So that was the deal, and everything was going along pretty well for a few days, except for the fact that every time Marwa caught sight of Mr. Norris, she stopped dead and stared at him like he was some kind of god. She was too scared to talk to him but too enthralled to walk away.

And that was exactly what was happening when Addie and Dickson got to Tish and Mr. Norris by the pond. Marwa was standing in front of him, her brown eyes as big as dinner plates. Addie could see it was making Mr. Norris grumpy and nervous.

Dickson pulled her away and led her up the hill to HVV.

"I'll catch up in a minute," Addie called to them.

She could hear Dickson telling Marwa that nobody, not even a superhero, likes to be stared at...as if it would make any difference to Marwa, Mr. Norris's number one fan.

"Hey, sweetie," said Tish, giving Addie a hug. "Great day, huh?"

Tish's phone rang.

She checked the screen.

"Oh...hold on," she said into the phone, biting her lip. She glanced at Mr. Norris with a question in her eyes.

He grumbled.

"Go ahead and take it. I'm fine here."

"I'm sorry, Mr. Norris, I'll just be a minute," she said, putting the phone to her ear and walking a few steps away.

Addie took off her backpack and squatted down by the pond. She ran her hand over the perfectly cut green grass, which came right up to the water's edge. Water bugs skittered across the surface, dodging the red and yellow leaves floating in lazy circles.

Tish had been talking in a low voice but suddenly hit some high notes.

"Really? It would be okay with you?"

Addie listened to a bit more of the conversation, then stood up.

She folded her arms in front of her.

"Well, that's it," she said.

"What is it?" said Mr. Norris.

"Tish. I think she's talking to one of her brothers. It sounds like we're moving."

Mr. Norris turned to Tish, but she was still on the phone. He turned back to Addie.

"You know," she said, looking up the hill toward HVV, "you never know how you feel about a place until you have to leave it. It kind of sneaks up on you when you're not looking."

She could feel him watching her, but he didn't say a word. He turned away with a disgusted throat-clearing. He began something that looked like breathing exercises. Addie heard him breathe in and in and in. It seemed like forever, then ever so slowly he breathed out. In and out, in and out, until Tish came bouncing back.

"Okay, sorry about that. It was a call I had to take. So, where to next, Mr. Norris? Shall we walk some more?"

"Wind's picked up," he grumbled. "I want to go back."

The wind had definitely picked up. It fanned out in ripples across the pond. It blew right through Addie's thin jacket.

Mr. Norris took off sharply up the hill with Tish by his side. Addie, dragging behind them, heard him talking to her in a low voice. A very determined low voice.

Her ears prickled when she heard her name.

"It's time.... You're not a girl anymore.... Think about Addie.... Mrs. Sloat ... But you have what it takes for the job...." He wasn't in his crazy, complaining mood. He was talking like he meant every word.

But Tish wasn't taking it lying down either.

"Not right for us…," she said. "Mrs. Sloat can't talk to me like that…. Can't live with Tina and Tim…"

They were coming up to the terrace door to Arborvine.

"Addie, go on in," said Mr. Norris. "I want to talk to your mother for another minute."

It was way more than a minute that they stood on the terrace talking, but Addie wasn't timing them. There was too much excitement going on in the lounge at Arborvine.

An enormous flower arrangement stood on the coffee table. It was almost as big as the giant-screen TV next to it. And in the center of the group clustered around it was Mrs. Firillo fluttering a white card.

"Read it again, Patsy," said Mrs. C.

"Well, let's see," Mrs. Firillo said, adjusting her glasses. "It says, 'Dear Mrs. Firillo, Please let me introduce myself. My name is Marcus Fox and I am your great-nephew, the son of your niece, Sandra, your sister Peggy's daughter. I'm afraid, since my parents died, I haven't kept up with family members as much as I'd like. Now, however, I'm new in town, having been offered a job on the news desk at the *City Journal*, and would very much like to come see you. Below is my contact information. I hope you will let me come visit you sometime soon. Best regards…'" She lowered the card. "Well!"

"Well!" said Mrs. C.

"Well, well, well!" said Mrs. A.

"Gorgeous flowers!" said Mrs. D.

"Do you want them in your room?" asked Wilma.

"Patsy, do you know who this person is?" said Gene Trippling.

Mrs. Firillo looked at the card again.

"He sent this photograph of himself." She studied the picture. "Peggy's grandson...I don't know whether I ever met him or not. I guess I must have at some point."

Mr. Trippling grumbled.

"It seems a little odd he's never gotten in touch before now. Maybe I'll get Dickson to look him up online."

"Oh, Gene, don't be so suspicious," said Mrs. D.

"Young people aren't always good about staying in touch," said Minerva, sitting on her scooter.

Gray heads nodded together.

"Still," said Wilma. "The flowers are to die for! Shall we put them in your room?"

"They'll barely fit!" muttered Mr. Trippling.

"Let's leave them here," said Mrs. Firillo, "so everyone can enjoy them."

"Oh, Patsy, this is so exciting!" said Mrs. A. "Just think, a reporter!"

The door from the terrace blew open and in came Tish and Mr. Norris, which meant the whole story had to be repeated for them.

Tish acted like she wasn't hearing a word. Chewing on her lip, full of impatience. Addie had seen the look before—every time Granny Lu had given Tish a talking-to about what she should be doing. Mr. Norris looked equally annoyed, especially with the blast of ladies chirping on about flowers in his face.

In the midst of the chatter, Minerva Swift waved Addie aside.

"Adelaide, can you come for brunch this Sunday? Your mother works on some Sundays, doesn't she? And I thought it would be fun for you." She cleared her throat. "I invited my niece and her husband, and they have a daughter who's about your age. You remember, the ones in the photograph?" She straightened the mail on her lap. "I would appreciate it if you could come."

"Um, I don't know."

"They go all out on the food—waffles, French toast, bacon, roast beef, desserts. There's a long buffet line, so you can pick whatever you want. Mrs. Sloat never comes, so it's quite festive. People get dressed up. "

"I don't know if my mom is working on Sunday."

"Well, why don't we ask her."

Minerva called to Tish and explained. Tish didn't care one way or another but finally agreed, as she could fit in an extra shift.

"And Mr. Norris, would you come too? Please, you won't regret it. It's the best meal of the week."

"Maybe. I'll see," he muttered.

After Minerva left, Addie said, "Tish, I really don't want to go. And I'll have to get dressed up."

Tish shrugged. "It'll be fun."

She wasn't convincing.

CHAPTER 17

Sunday morning, Tish and Addie got off the bus and walked up the drive. It was lucky that HVV was on one of the major roads stretching out from Philadelphia. There were stores nearby, a shopping center next door, and a bus stop right at the entrance, which made commuting from Aunt Tina and Uncle Tim's easy.

On this particular morning, however, Bella hadn't wanted Addie to leave and was on her way to a meltdown when Aunt Tina sidetracked her by saying they would go out for breakfast. And Addie promised to bring back some goodies from the brunch that she could hide for Bella in their ongoing treasure hunt game.

As they walked up the drive, Addie wasn't sure what she was getting into. She pulled at her itchy lace collar.

"I feel stupid in these clothes," she said. She hadn't gotten this dressed up since Granny Lu's funeral. And she had only worn a dress then because Mrs. Donald, one of Granny Lu's clients, had made one especially for her.

Marwa had taken it upon herself to style Addie for Sunday brunch.

"Don't worry, Addie, I get you all fixed up," said Marwa, with a gleam in her eyes. "You know, you are very smart about almost everything, but clothes..." She looked up from Addie's worn-out jeans, "I help you."

And that is how Addie came to be wearing a short pink skirt with three tiered ruffles and a black sweater with the itchy lace collar. Black tights and Addie's black sneakers completed the outfit. Marwa was willing to loan Addie her hairband with the big white flower on the side, but Addie got out of that one.

"You look great, sweetie," said Tish. "Marwa knows her stuff."

Tish had been in a bad mood for days, ever since her conversation with Mr. Norris. She didn't want to talk about it. Granny Lu would have said she was "down in the dumps." But then, Sunday morning, for some reason, her world was brighter.

At the top of the drive, the road forked one way to Arborvine and the nursing facility, the other to the main entrance. They followed the road to Arborvine until Tish stopped and turned to Addie.

"So, I've made a decision," she said.

Addie waited.

"You know, the problem with Mrs. Sloat and all... Well, I was feeling like I didn't belong here. I know they still don't like me. But I was feeling like everything was just kind of all-around bad here. And, of course, living with Tim and Tina isn't easy."

She paused.

"You know, sometimes I think things could be better for us someplace else."

"Yeah, I know," said Addie, looking down at the asphalt.

"So, I was all set to leave...."

"Yeah."

"Yeah, well. Mr. Norris..." Tish's eyes rolled and she shook her head. "He can be a blister, but he got me thinking." She fixed the collar on Addie's sweater. "Anyway, see his house over there, and the garage? Well, he said we could have the apartment over the garage."

Addie stared at the garage, taking the idea in.

"What do you think?" said Tish.

"Good. I guess."

"He said we could try it. For a month. Well, that is if the Sloat keeps me on past the next couple of weeks. I could take more shifts," said Tish. "Or at least, take the ones I wanted without worrying about you and transportation. You'd be right next door. I think it'd make things a whole lot easier and better for us. And by the time the month's up, I'd know if I really wanted to stay here or not."

"Wow, we could have our own place," said Addie.

"Yes, we could."

Addie gave Tish a hug.

"Let's do it, then."

Minerva was right about Sunday brunch. It was like a big party. People were lined up outside the big main dining room in their Sunday best. There were cornstalks and Halloween decorations around the door. Every table had fall-colored flowers on the tables...and then there was the food.

No sooner had they sat down at their table than they had to get up and go to the soup-and-salad bar for a first course. Then they had to go through the main buffet line before the roast beef was all gone. Des was at the meat-carving station and gave Addie one of the end slices. Then, before the best desserts were taken, they had to visit the dessert table. By the time they finally sat down to eat, every inch of the white linen tablecloth was jammed tight with plates of fabulous food.

Minerva's niece, Mrs. Blevins, and her husband took turns getting plates for Minerva, who had parked her scooter outside the dining room and sat at the table like a queen.

Addie didn't know where to start. She had waffles and bacon on one side of her, roast beef and mashed potatoes on the other, broccoli salad up around eleven o'clock, and a slice of gooey chocolate cake wedged in at one o'clock. She noticed Mr. Norris, on her left, digging into his roast beef. He almost looked happy. Lily, Minerva's great-niece, was on her right, picking through a mountain of greens topped with a few bits of chicken.

"Is that all you're having?" said Addie.

"Mmm-hmm." Lily nodded. "I'm on my school's varsity field hockey team and it looks like we could win the Havens Cup this year, so I'm basically in training until Thanksgiving."

"Wow," Addie said, looking between her plates and Lily's plate of green leaves, "that's too bad. I guess you can't wait for Thanksgiving!"

Lily looked at her.

"The Havens Cup is a really big deal. Do you play sports?"

"Nah, I basically come over here after school every day till my mom gets off work."

Lily's eyebrows did an up and down. "That sounds a little grim."

"Oh, it's not too bad," said Mr. Norris, working through his roast beef, "she gets to spend time with people like me."

That put a stop to Lily. Her shoulders gave a "who cares" twitch or two as she plunged back into the depths of her salad.

"Hey," Addie said so only Mr. Norris could hear. "Tish told me about the apartment." She pushed a whole strip of bacon into her mouth. "Thanks."

"Well, it's no use to me. Might as well fill it with someone." He put down his knife and fork. "But no snooping. Hear me? You and your little gang are not allowed to go anywhere else. The ground floor of the garage is strictly off-limits. Understood?"

Addie nodded. "Got it."

She could feel those dark eyes of his staying on her. "I said I got it! Hey, I wonder if there's any hot sauce around here?"

"Adelaide," said Mrs. Blevins, "Minerva tells me she's been enjoying reading *The Wind in the Willows* with you. The classics are wonderful, aren't they? I wish Lily had read more of them."

Addie thought she heard a snicker from Lily.

Mrs. Blevins wasn't done. "And what a cute outfit that is. Lily, we should look for a sweater like that for you."

"It's my friend Marwa's," said Addie, working on bites of waffle. "She loaned me the outfit. She's into clothes."

Mrs. Blevins smiled.

"Well, she has taste, I'd say. You know, you and Lily look to be about the same size, and Lily, your closets are packed. Addie, would you ever like some things Lily doesn't wear anymore?"

Addie didn't know what to say, and anyway, she had a mouthful of food.

Minerva looked annoyed as she cut in. "Well, I can talk to Adelaide and her mother about that later. Would anyone like another dessert?"

Mr. Norris gave Addie a nudge.

"Adelaide," he said with a sly snicker, "who's that with Patsy Firillo?"

Addie followed where Mr. Norris was looking. A table away sat Mrs. Firillo and a young guy all done up in a suit and tie. Addie had been too busy with the feast, but once she paid attention, it wasn't hard to hear them.

"I bet it's that great-nephew of hers. The one who sent the flowers."

"Hmph," grumbled Mr. Norris. "For someone who hasn't been interested in her at all, he certainly seems interested now."

Mrs. Firillo was answering one question after another from the guy about how and when she came to Happy Valley, what living at HVV was like, and how HVV was started, when she noticed Mr. Norris looking her way.

"Mr. Norris!" She waved before turning back to the man. "His family is the one I'm telling you about. They owned this whole estate before Happy Valley bought it. He still lives here on the property. Come and meet him."

She heaved herself up and brought her guest over to their table.

"Minerva, Mr. Norris, so sorry to interrupt," said Mrs. Firillo. "But I wanted to introduce my great-nephew, Marcus Fox." She put her hand to her heart. "He's the one who sent the beautiful flowers." Something caught Addie's eye, but she couldn't say anything in the middle of the brunch. It would have to wait.

Everyone nodded at Mrs. Firillo and smiled. Except Mr. Norris.

"I was telling him about how Happy Valley started, Mr. Norris. That it had been in your family since...oh my goodness, I don't know how long.'

"1784," said Mr. Norris, eyeing both of them.

"Really?" said Marcus Fox, impressed. "What a history! I've recently taken a job at the *City Journal,* and I'm learning just how much history there is in this area. I'd love to hear more about your family sometime, if you wouldn't mind, Mr. Norris."

Marcus Fox flashed a big, wide, waiting smile. He had brown eyes with long lashes like a puppy dog. His chin had just the right amount of neatly trimmed stubble. He looked like the friendliest person in the world. Addie didn't like him one bit.

"Minerva, I hate to say it," said Mrs. Blevins, depositing her napkin on the table, "but we really should be going. Lily has practice at three."

Mrs. Firillo and Marcus Fox wandered back to their table, Mrs. Firillo introducing Marcus to everyone she could see.

"There's something about that Marcus Fox," muttered Mr. Norris under his breath. "He looks familiar."

The Blevinses gathered their things and got busy saying "How nice...," "How lovely...," "I hope we can do this again...." Lily stretched her neck from side to side. Addie wrapped little pastries in a napkin for Bella and the last bit of beef in another napkin for Fluffy.

After everyone had gone and Mr. Norris had stumped on ahead back to his room, Addie was finally able to get Minerva alone.

"Can you check out the pearls Mrs. Firillo is wearing? They kind of look like the ones Mrs. Barker used to wear."

CHAPTER 18

Addie had to admit Minerva Swift was a smooth operator. On Monday afternoon, the very next day, Addie heard how Mrs. Sloat had arrived in her office that morning to find a note from Dr. Barker saying Genevieve Barker had found her pearls. With no other information, the Sloat immediately called Dr. Barker for details.

"Excellent news, isn't it," said Dr. Barker on the phone. "They were in her room all the time. Behind a book or something, I was told."

"Who told you?"

"One of the nurses. I think it was Minerva Swift who finally found them."

"No mention of Tish or anyone else involved?"

"No, that's all I heard."

Mrs. Sloat wasn't happy unless she could blame someone for things that went wrong, so she marched down to Arborvine.

Wilma was there, and Wilma always knew everything.

"That's right, Mrs. Sloat, they were behind a book. Funny, huh? Why would anyone put their pearls behind a book? But you know Mrs. Barker forgets things a little bit, so who knows how they got there. The good thing is that they are now where they need to be—around her neck."

"Well, I'm happy they were found."

But Mrs. Sloat didn't look happy. She went off to find Minerva Swift.

"Ms. Swift?" said Mrs. Sloat, knocking on her door. "Are you in? It's Melinda Sloat."

Minerva, who had been sitting in her sunny window enjoying the peace and quiet, put down her book and explained how she had found Genevieve's pearls.

"I was looking for something to read to her and found them in her bookshelf."

"And did she say how they got there?"

Minerva shook her head.

"She didn't know, but she was certainly glad to have them back. A mystery solved."

"Mmm, yes, wonderful," said Mrs. Sloat. "Well, thank you," she added, leaving.

Minerva leaned back in her easy chair and smiled.

The real story was the talk of Arborvine that afternoon.

"Oh, you should have seen her! Sorry, Dickson, but you know how your mother gets worked up," said Wilma. "She was sure someone"—Wilma glanced at Addie—"had taken those pearls."

"It's all thanks to Minerva and Gene," said Mrs. A.

Now that their dear friend Mrs. B had passed away, the three ladies couldn't play cards till they found a fourth, so they spent a lot more time in the lounge.

"Minerva said you'd spotted the pearls, Addie. Smart girl!" said Mrs. D. "Minerva talked to Gene...."

"And wasn't he sweet to Patsy!" said Mrs. B. "He recognized right away they weren't hers. He persuaded Patsy there was something wrong with the clasp, so she took them off, and while he was looking at it, Minerva asked her about the photograph Marcus Fox had given her, and before you know it, Patsy was off and running."

"Never gave the pearls another thought!" said Mrs. D.

"How did she get them in the first place?" said Addie.

"Who knows?" said Wilma. "She forgets where she's going every now and then. Ah, Mr. Trippling. We were just talking about you."

Mr. Trippling came down the hall carrying a grocery bag.

"Only lovely compliments, I hope."

"They were saying how nice you were to Mrs. Firillo about the pearls," said Dickson.

"Oh, well," he said, putting down the bag. "She would have been terribly embarrassed about it if she knew. She just gets a little mixed up."

"Don't we all," said Mrs. C.

Everyone nodded.

"I just don't want them to move her to the memory care facility, so thank you all for covering for her. Is she in her room, do you know?"

"She and Marwa took Izzy for a walk," said Wilma.

"Oh, good," said Mr. Trippling. "Well, I brought her some ice cream. A little fudge swirl always does the trick."

"Or you could just show her that photo of the nephew," said Wilma, with a laugh. "She goes on and on about him!"

"And really, I'm not sure why," said Mr. Trippling, looking annoyed. "She's only known him for what, five minutes?"

"Oh, now," said Mrs. D, "it's something fun for her to think about."

"But she doesn't remember ever meeting him..."

"Yes, but we know she forgets things," said Mrs. A.

"...and now she says he looks exactly like her sister. I just think it's unusual, to say the least," said Mr. Trippling, stumping off to the kitchenette.

"Well, ladies," said Wilma to the group that was left, "the mystery of the disappearing pearls has been solved. What'll we get excited about next?"

"Tell Addie about Mrs. Sloat hearing they're moving to the apartment over Mr. Norris's garage!"

"Oh, yeah, that's a good one." Wilma grinned. "Especially when she realized there was nothing she could do about it!"

✳

When Tish was done with work, she, Addie, and Mr. Norris walked over to his house to get the key to the apartment. Mr. Norris used only one cane now and hardly ever needed it. Addie suspected he liked the look of it more than anything and the fact that he could use it to bang on doors, or things...or people.

Behind his kitchen door there were rows of keys on hooks.

"Let's see," he said, leafing through the tags on the keys. "Old safe-deposit box, big leather suitcase, small leather suitcase, metal file, clock in hall, I haven't used most of these in years. Ahh, chauffeur's apartment. Here we go." He handed Tish a key. "I only see the one key. Can you get a copy made? I should have an extra one here."

"Sure, and I'd like Addie to have her own key," said Tish. "So can I get a couple of copies made?"

"Fine with me," he said. "Whatever you two work out. Oh, one other thing," he said as they went out and he locked the door. "Don't forget to take the cat."

"Aww, Mr. Norris, you sure you don't want to keep her?" said Tish.

"Very funny."

As they walked back to Arborvine, Mr. Norris tapped Addie on the shoulder with his cane.

"You remember what I said about not snooping in the garage?"

"Yup, I remember," said Addie carefully.

"I'm trusting you," he said.

"Don't worry. I hear you."

The trouble is, if someone tells you there is one place, only one place, absolutely only one place, you are never, ever allowed to go, it only makes you more and more curious about what's there.

CHAPTER
19

Addie had to hand it to Aunt Tina. One good thing about having a super-organized person in the family is that, when it comes to moving, cleaning, and finding furniture for a new apartment, they are exactly the person you want to have around. Aunt Tina and Uncle Tim, her brother, Matt, who worked at HVV, and his wife helped Tish and Addie clean the place from top to bottom the next Sunday morning. That same afternoon, while Tina took Tish to the supermarket in the shopping center next door, Tim and Matt brought over a table and chairs from Goodwill, a sofa from the Come and Get It hallway at HVV (Matt got the okay from the building and grounds department), and two beds from a discount furniture place. And after collecting Fluffy, they were moved.

Tish and Addie were collapsed on their new sofa

when Uncle Tim came back up the outside stairs to the apartment.

"Almost forgot this," he said. He held out an envelope to Addie. "Tina found this when she was going through the old stuff we have in our basement from Granny Lu. She was looking for anything you could use over here, and there was a box of papers and books. This has your name on it, Addie. Sorry we didn't find it until now."

Inside the envelope were a few photographs. One was of Addie and Granny Lu the day their matching rainbow leggings arrived in the mail. Another was a picture of Addie sitting in front of the pink Christmas tree opening a present from one of the clients. And the last was of Granny Lu and Addie when Addie was little, maybe about Bella's age. Addie was standing in front of Granny Lu, who was sitting on the floor, and they were laughing and rubbing noses.

Addie didn't know what to say. There were a couple of photos of Granny Lu in Uncle Tim and Aunt Tina's house, but Addie didn't have any of her own. Until now.

Tish, looking at the pictures over her shoulder, gave her a squeeze.

Something was knotted up at the back of Addie's throat, but she managed to say, "Thanks," in a small voice. "Did you...find the box Granny Lu and I kept?"

"That box you asked me about?" said Uncle Tim. He shook his head. "No, sorry."

He pulled Addie and Tish into a big hug.

"We're going to miss you girls, but I'm glad you have

a place and it's nearby." He pointed at Tish. "Check your schedule this week and as soon as you have a free evening, come over for dinner." He looked at his watch. "We have to go pick up the kids. Boy, Bella and Logan are sure going to miss you, Addie."

"Yeah," she said, "I'm going to miss them, too. Tell Bella we'll have her over here for a play date soon."

"You got it," he said. "She would love that."

It was after he left and Addie was putting the pictures back in the envelope that she saw a folded piece of paper tucked inside. She recognized Granny Lu's handwriting immediately.

She put the envelope away till Tish had gone over to Arborvine to put in a little overtime and help with dinner.

Sitting at the new kitchen table, Addie smoothed the paper out. She hadn't seen Granny Lu's handwriting in a long time. A note at the top of the page read:

Dear Addie,

It's a gorgeous day here, sunny and warm... just the kind of fall day I love, though I'm not feeling too energized today. I want to be sure our Dream Box is safe no matter what, so I got a great idea and buried it! All our treasures are still inside, and you will find it someday. Here's a map! Not as good as one of yours, but I think it will work.

I hope you and Tish are having fun on your camping trip. Hope you come home soon.

Love, love, love, XOXOXO Granny Lu

Addie bent over the paper, tears mixed with excitement bubbling up inside. The Dream Box had been safe all along? Leave it to good old Granny Lu to think of everything. And to come up with a treasure hunt for it!

Below the note was a map. It was a map of Granny Lu's house, all right, because she'd labeled everything. She'd even put her address on it. Addie ran her finger over every line: the short driveway leading to the ranch house and garage, the flagpole, the lilac bush with the gnome house under it, the rosebush, the bird feeder, the birdbath, and the little wishing well covering up the well connection. Distances were marked off in feet.

Addie looked up. Did Granny Lu really go out there with a tape measure and measure everything? Yup—Addie smiled; she could picture her doing exactly that. She'd do it even if she wasn't feeling well, because those commemorative coins and stamps, as she always said, would be worth a ton of money someday.

Addie checked the map again. As on any good treasure map, there was a nice big black X. It was about halfway between the wishing well and the birdbath and a certain number of feet from the house. If it was still there, Addie would find it.

Carefully, she refolded the paper and held it against her cheek. "Thanks, Granny Lu," she whispered, before tucking the envelope into her map notebook. She felt better knowing that somehow, someday, she would get herself back to Mount Repose, Maine. It was as close as she could get to having a map back to Granny Lu herself.

She flipped through her notebook when she saw one

of the first maps she'd ever made with Granny Lu. It was of their little dead-end street.

"A cul-de-sac," Granny Lu had said, "if you want to be fancy."

Granny Lu had drawn lines for the road and driveways; Addie had put in squares for the houses. They had gotten out a box of crayons, and together they'd colored in bushes and trees, cars, swing sets, and dogs.

While they worked, Granny Lu had told her about the places they would go someday.

"Ms. Schmidt just came back from visiting her son in New York City. We should go to New York City someday, though she said the subway went like a bat out of hell!" They had laughed and laughed at that, even though Addie hadn't known what it meant then.

"Or how about Paris, or India, or"—Granny Lu had thought a minute, then had put her face close to Addie's and whispered, "the moo—oon!"

Granny Lu had sighed happily.

"You know why maps are fun, Addie? They're all about adventure! Sometimes they're places we know, like our road, and sometimes they're places we haven't gotten to yet. And those new places can be strange, sure, maybe even weird and uncomfortable, but"—she'd whispered again—"they can be thrilling!"

Addie remembered getting upset because her houses hadn't looked the way she'd wanted them to look. She saw the creases in the paper where she'd started to crumple it up before Granny Lu had stopped her.

"Whoa, what are you doing?"

"The houses aren't right!"

"Oh, come on now, they're fine. Maps aren't perfect. Goodness, some of those early maps I've seen had it all wrong! Maps are just guides. Sometimes they get it right, sometimes they don't."

Granny Lu had smoothed her hair.

"Maps are only there to help show us the way...if we want to use them." Was Addie imagining it, or did she have a dim memory of Tish showing up around that time, and Granny Lu saying softly, "And some of us need to find our own way."

CHAPTER 20

I'm so excited!" Marwa couldn't stop herself from skipping all the way to Mr. Norris's house. It was the first afternoon after Addie and Tish had moved into their new apartment.

"I just have to put this key back in Mr. Norris's house, and then I'll show you the apartment," said Addie. She unlocked the kitchen door and put the extra apartment key Tish had gotten made on the hooks behind the door.

"Wow, that's a lot of keys," said Dickson. He tilted his head sideways to read the tags. "Storage box, attic, gray metal box, padlock..."

There was another key Addie had her eye on. She'd noticed it the day before when she and Tish and Mr. Norris were there. A key with a tag that read GARAGE. She'd pushed it out of her mind then, and she pushed it out now.

"Okay, let's go," she said.

"Wait," said Dickson. He looked at them with such a gleam in his eyes, it was like both Addie and Marwa knew instantly what he was thinking.

"We have to see if it's there," he said in a husky voice. "Come on, we have to."

"He's right," Marwa said, looking at Addie. "Where did your mother say? A closet in the bedroom?"

They didn't wait for an answer but darted off looking for a bedroom. There wasn't one on the ground floor. The two of them flew upstairs with Addie close behind.

Four bedrooms. Each with a closet.

"I'll take this one," said Dickson, disappearing into a room.

Addie and Marwa each took other rooms. There was silence for a few minutes until they met back in the hall.

"Well," said Dickson, looking at their blank faces. "One more room."

Dickson and Marwa dove for the closet in the last bedroom. There wasn't really room for a third. Addie took in the rest of the room. This had to be Mr. Norris's bedroom. It was weird just like he was. The walls were covered in funky wallpaper and hung with old prints of dirigibles, the Eiffel Tower, and designs for race cars. An old leather chair with its bottom falling out had a worn teddy bear perched on one arm, a tangle of old shoelaces on the other. Books and magazines, extra batteries, packages of socks were piled up on the floor against every wall. She was looking at a few old photographs on the bureau when Dickson came out with a gargly, strangled shriek.

"That's...it!"

Marwa whistled.

Addie went and leaned over them.

The blue suit was the color of an early morning in May if there were ice crystals glittering in the air. Marwa pulled it slowly up out of the box as if she was holding on to a dream come true. The silver streamers floated away down the back.

"Wow, what do you know," said Addie, under her breath. "He didn't get rid of it." It was kind of a shock that maybe he'd listened to her and thought twice about throwing it away.

Dickson was still on his knees.

"Look" was all he said, lifting up the heavy belt.

Out of the silver clouds on the belt buckle shone a bright *B* in a sunburst of raised metal. There were figures on either side of the *B*, their cheeks full of air blowing toward it.

No one said anything.

"I can't believe it," whispered Marwa finally.

"Me either," said Dickson.

Addie was ready to snap out of it. "Come on, we better put it back. Really carefully too. Make it look just like it was. You want to see the apartment, right?"

She made sure everything was put back as if they'd never been there. Marwa and Dickson moved in a kind of trance as they went downstairs and out the door. Before Addie locked up, though, she paused.

"What is it?" asked Dickson.

"Wait a second," she said. She was thinking hard.

Oh, come on, she thought. Might as well go all the way and see just how crazy he was.

She reached behind the door, grabbed the key marked GARAGE, and stuffed it in her pocket.

Climbing the outside stairs of the garage and checking out their new apartment took less than a minute. Saying hello to Fluffy took way longer and was way more interesting.

"Maybe I could come hang out here after school," said Marwa, trying to coax the cat out from under a bed. "Then I could play with Fluff."

"And if I was here," said Dickson, "then I wouldn't have to sit in Mrs. Firillo's storage compartment." He thought. "Nah, I need to use Mr. Trippling's laptop when I'm not helping him with his stuff. Boy, wait till I find out more about that suit!"

While the three of them sat on the floor listening to Fluffy growl, Addie had her hand in her pocket, twisting the garage key around and around in her fingers.

"Hey," she said. She slowly held up the key. "Know what this is? I think it's the key for that door." She pointed to a door at the other end of the apartment. It wasn't an outside door, so it had to be a door leading down into the garage.

Dickson's eyes opened wide and blinked.

"But I thought you said Mr. Norris said..."

Addie nodded. "He did, I know. But we just found the suit and...should we...do you think...just take a peek?"

"Ooo, a peek! Yes, yes!" squealed Marwa.

"We'll open the door and look. That's all," said Addie. "Promise?"

They nodded. Marwa was so excited she was twitching.

Addie put her ear to the door. So did the others.

Nothing.

She pushed the key into the lock and turned it. The door opened with a rusty, protesting wail. Fluffy hissed from under the bed.

They were at the top of a flight of stairs going down into a huge cavern of a garage. Because the windows in the curved garage doors were covered over with paper, the only light came from their apartment and from places where the paper was torn and curling away from the windows.

They leaned over the railing at the top of the stairs.

"We need Brad with his flashlights right now," said Dickson.

The longer they stood and looked, though, the more their eyes adjusted and what was in the garage came to life.

One of the garage bays was empty, another had an old station wagon that Addie guessed belonged to Mr. Norris, and the other was piled high with tarps. Along the far wall was an area like a workshop with tools hanging on the wall and over a workbench.

"I wonder what's in that door over there in the corner," said Dickson, pointing. "It looks heavy-duty. Like a bank vault or something." He turned to Addie. "Okay if I go down as long as I stay on the stairs?"

"Me too," said Marwa. "It smells so good in here. My dad had a garage in Iraq. I love this place."

Addie thought of Mr. Norris's eyes. But they were just looking, and there wasn't all that much to see anyway. It couldn't make any difference whether they were on this step or that one.

"You can go down the stairs, but not a single step farther." She didn't sound like herself. She knew Mr. Norris trusted her, but she told herself she was being so careful that he wouldn't really mind.

That was, until Fluffy decided to shoot past her down the stairs and disappear into the shadows.

Addie panicked. She could hear Mr. Norris yelling, "THAT BLASTED CAT!" as if he was towering over her.

What could they do but charge down the stairs and hunt for Fluffy, searching behind boxes, rooting around in every shadowy corner? What if they couldn't find her? What if she went to the bathroom and made the whole place stink?

Addie was in so much trouble, she didn't hear Dickson at first. It took Marwa squeaking to make her pay attention.

Dickson had waded into the pile of tarps and pulled one aside. Fluffy had found her way underneath them and was growling. He tunneled in and grabbed her. That was when he discovered what else was underneath. It wasn't just a pile of tarps, it was a few tarps covering something up. Something low and long and sleek.

Dickson, with Fluffy clutched under one arm, pulled off more of the cover, staggering back under its weight.

No one moved.

The shining sky-blue tail fin of a car sparkled in the gloom. It cut into the air as sharp and shiny as a knife point, with a space-age red taillight at the tip. It was fantastic, it was crazy, it was the coolest thing ever, it was...

They pulled off more of the tarp.

None of them had ever seen anything like it.

"This doesn't look like WWE," said Dickson, taking extra breaths. "This looks...almost...like a superhero's—"

"What did I TELL you!" shouted Marwa, jumping up and down.

CHAPTER 21

"Des knows all about cars, maybe we can ask him what it is!" said Dickson.

The three of them were back in Addie's apartment after capturing Fluffy and making sure there were no signs they'd been downstairs in the garage.

They were still dazed from the sight of the crazy blue car.

"We can't tell Des," said Addie. "We can't have Mr. Norris finding out we were there. He'd kill us."

Marwa sighed a long, dreamy sigh.

"I wonder what it looks like when it's out in the open."

"I bet Des would go insane if he saw it," said Dickson.

When Des wasn't working at HVV, going to school, or cooking for his family at home, his favorite thing was working on his old Honda. He'd taken it apart twice, built it back together twice, but there was still a mysterious clunking sound deep in the engine that bothered him.

Addie was thinking hard.

"You know," she said, "there's the other car in there that I bet belongs to Mr. Norris. If it's his, sooner or later he's going to need somebody to check it over for him. Either he's going to start driving again or he'll have to sell it. What if I told Mr. Norris sometime that Des likes working on old cars. Maybe it could get Des in there and we could find out something."

A few loud knocks came from downstairs.

Marwa's eyes grew three sizes larger.

Addie looked at both of them.

"We put everything back down there, didn't we?"

"Could it be Mr. Norris?" said Dickson in a whispery squeak.

Fluffy hissed under the bed.

The three of them stood in the apartment, not making a sound. Addie shoved the garage key down deep in her jeans pocket.

They waited.

"Maybe, whoever it was, they've gone," whispered Addie.

Then, in the same second, the breath of all three caught in their throats as footsteps sounded on the outside stairs. Someone was coming up to the apartment.

All they could do was stare at the window of the apartment door.

Addie was dreading the sight of Mr. Norris's long,

grizzled hair and his angry black eyes. But it wasn't him. It was a young and friendly face. Marcus Fox.

He smiled as soon as he saw them and waved.

"Who's that?" said Dickson.

"It's Marcus Fox," said Addie. "Mrs. Firillo's great-nephew."

She went and opened the door.

"Hey! Hi," he said. "It's Addie, right?"

His big, bright smile showed off the whitest teeth Addie had ever seen.

"Look, I'm really sorry to bother you. I was looking for Mr. Norris. He wasn't over at Arborvine, and they said he might be around here taking a walk." He didn't wait for an answer. "Hi," he said, holding up a hand to wave to Dickson and Marwa. "I'm Marcus Fox. I'm related to Patsy Firillo, and I met Mr. Norris the other day at brunch. I was hoping I could catch up with him to learn more about the history of this place."

"I'm Marwa." Marwa beamed up at him with stars in her eyes.

Dickson played it cool and professional.

"I'm Dickson. I can probably tell you some stuff about the place."

"Really? Wow, that would be great. I'm working for the *City Journal* and I've come across some really fascinating information. Actually, are you guys free?" He looked at Addie. "Could we talk outside for a minute?"

She had barely nodded when he turned and led the way back down the stairs.

"I heard you and your mom moved in here," he said

when they reached the courtyard. He was looking the whole place over. "That'll make it super convenient for her and her job, right?

"Hey, Dickson," he said, bringing his attention back to them, "maybe you can help me with something. I found out there may have been a research laboratory somewhere here that Mr. Norris's father built back in the 1940s. Have you heard about that?"

Dickson's eyes bulged.

"A research lab? Here?"

"Yeah, I know! Cool, huh?" said Marcus Fox. "You kids probably haven't heard of the Manhattan Project."

"THE Manhattan Project?" Dickson blurted out. "Of course I've heard of it! Developing the first atomic bombs they used in World War Two!" If he could have grabbed Marcus Fox and shaken him, he would have. "Wait, are you saying some of the research happened HERE?"

Marcus Fox lifted his eyebrows and smiled.

"No way!" Dickson was trying to catch his breath.

"Was it dangerous?" asked Addie.

Marcus Fox's smile vanished.

"That's what I'd like to find out."

Dickson had been concentrating on something. He suddenly looked at Addie and Marwa in a state of wonder. "That's what's behind that metal door, I bet!"

"A metal door?" asked Marcus Fox softly.

"Yeah," said Dickson, ignoring Addie's look of alarm. "It's like the door of a vault. Downstairs in the garage."

Addie cut in quickly.

"We heard about it from Mr. Norris, but we're not allowed to go in there. Ever. And we haven't."

Marwa nodded up and down.

"Wow, I would really like to see what's in there," Marcus Fox said, looking at the big garage doors. "But I guess I'll have to talk to Mr. Norris about that."

"And anyway," said Addie, "we don't even have the key."

Her hands were in her pockets, her right hand touching the jagged edges of the key.

"Boy, the Manhattan Project!" said Dickson. "I've been doing my own research online but haven't come up with any mention of that."

"Hey," said Marcus Fox. "Maybe we could work together. I could share the sites I use and you could show me what you've found." He laughed. "You know, my sister's son is a computer whiz. He uses a crazy online username....What is it..."

"Yeah, I do too," said Dickson, with a cool, computer-whiz kind of shrug. "I use my WWE alias. The Platinum Python!"

Marcus Fox gave an outsized laugh.

"Wow, impressive. I love it!"

"And boy, do I have more research to do now!" said Dickson. "The Manhattan Project and the blue ca—"

"Dickson!" Addie cried louder than she meant to, but it did the trick. Dickson realized he was about to say way too much.

They stood awkwardly in the silence that followed.

"Well, kids, gosh, thanks for talking to me," said

Marcus Fox, with his usual grin back in place. "You've been a big help. And who knows, maybe you and I can help each other out, Dickson. Bye, Marwa, nice to meet you. And congratulations again on the apartment, Addie. It looks great. See you guys!"

They watched him cross the parking lot and head toward HVV.

"Dickson, you almost said something about the car!" Addie hissed at him. "And you said way too much about the garage! What were you thinking?"

He couldn't look her in the eye.

She went on, trying to make both of them understand.

"We have to be really, really careful! For Mr. Norris's sake. He doesn't want anyone to know any of this. We already know more than he'd like."

"Marcus Fox sure is good-looking," said Marwa.

"Marwa, did you hear what I said?"

Marwa turned back to them.

"Of course I heard." She clasped her hands. "But this is all so exciting!"

Addie sighed.

"Dickson, what time is it?"

"Almost five. We need to go meet our moms." They turned toward HVV. "Addie, you don't have to go back, now that you live here," said Dickson.

"I know, but I might as well walk over with you guys. I told Minerva I'd read with her after dinner and, maybe if I go now, I can talk Tish into letting me get dinner in the employees' cafeteria."

"You're so lucky you live here," said Marwa.

"Yeah, and just think," said Dickson, "you live right above the garage." He looked at Addie. "You have to admit at least that the car is amazing. I can't wait to go online to see what I can find out."

"Dickson," said Marwa, pulling on his sleeve to stop him. "See if you can find out what his superpowers are."

"Guys—" said Addie, trying to stop them.

"Wait!" said Dickson, waving an arm to shush her. "Wait a minute. I remember reading in comics how sometimes ordinary people get powers from superheroes...."

He turned to face them. His eyes were the size of baseballs.

"What if I got some superpower from Mr. Norris," he said to himself. "Think what the kids at school would say. Wow, think what I could do at lunch!"

"How would you get his superpowers?" said Marwa.

Dickson stared off into the distance.

"In stories, you have to get something from the person." He banged his head with his hand. "I've got his handkerchief! Remember?" Dickson's voice rose higher and higher. "He gave it to me when he found us at his house!"

"But," said Addie, frowning, "you've had it for days and it hasn't done anything for you yet, has it?"

"True," said Dickson. "But maybe I haven't used it in the right way."

"Dickson, where is it?" cried Marwa.

"In my backpack at Arborvine."

Marwa barely let him finish before she was pulling him by the sleeve.

"Come on, let's get it!"

They ran off toward Arborvine, leaving Addie standing in the middle of a parking lot.

She felt as if her world was spinning into a whirl of useless dreams, of what-ifs, like a bunch of colored balloons, each one pulling at its string, wanting to lift her away. She stood perfectly still on the asphalt, trying to feel the pull of gravity, willing it to hold her tight and tethered to the ground.

CHAPTER 22

When walkers were called to dismiss the next day at school, Addie and Marwa ran into Dickson in the hallway outside his classroom. As he left, they could hear kids calling out, "Bye, Dickson! See you tomorrow!"

They'd never heard that before. Ivy and Janelle were with them. All four girls looked at Dickson, as he walked along smiling to himself.

"What's up with you?" asked Addie as they headed downstairs.

Dickson shrugged.

"Not much," he said with a big grin.

The four of them kept pestering him for more information as they rounded the corner by the library, passed the art room, the music room, and the cafeteria, but he wouldn't saying one word. Dickson could be really annoying sometimes.

Outside, Ivy and Janelle gave up and went on their way. Dickson started toward the path to HVV, but as soon as they were past the playground and out of sight of any teachers, he whipped out a king-sized candy bar from his pocket.

"Guess who gave me this?" he said with a super-satisfied smile, holding it up the way an Olympic athlete holds up a gold medal.

He paused, then let it out. "Marshall, that's who!"

Marshall, the bully of bullies, was also the coolest kid in Dickson's fourth grade. If anyone else dyed their hair green or wore vomit-yellow basketball shorts, it would be a disaster. If Marshall did it, it was super cool, and every kid would go home that night begging for green hair dye and yellow basketball shorts.

"What happened?" said Addie.

"Come on. I'll tell you two on the way," Dickson said, strutting off to the path through the trees. He sounded different...like he was suddenly in charge or something. He even walked differently. There was a relaxed kind of...swagger, that was what it was.

Marwa looked at Addie.

"Dickson," Marwa said, catching up to him. "Tell us!"

"Okay," he said, grinning and turning around to them. He was back to the old Dickson. "You...will... never...believe...what...happened!" He bounced up and down. "I got it! I got the superpower!" He did a jerky victory dance all his own.

"So, we go to lunch. Of course, it had to be Sloppy Joe day. The worst! Do you have any idea what it's like on Sloppy Joe day under the lunch tables? And Marshall and his gang come over to shove me under and...ha, this is the best part!" He looked Addie and Marwa straight in the eye. "I said 'No thanks.' That was it. 'No thanks.'" Dickson did another victory dance.

"That was it?" said Addie.

"What—" Marwa began.

"Oh, and then I punched him," said Dickson.

"Who!" Addie and Marwa cried together.

"Lucas, one of Marshall's pack. Ha! You should have seen them. They let me eat lunch. At the table!"

"Did you get in trouble?"

"Oh, yeah, I got sent to the principal's office, and I have to stay home tomorrow. It was so worth it. Then Marshall gave me the candy bar. He said I was kind of cool. Crazy, huh?"

He stopped in the middle of the path.

"But don't you see?" he said in a hush. "It MEANS I've gotten some of Mr. Norris's SUPERPOWER!"

"Oh, Dickson," said Marwa, her eyes shining. "What if I touch you—would I get some too?" She laid a finger on his arm.

Addie frowned. "Dickson, do you really feel different?"

Marwa touched him again.

"I don't feel any different," she said.

"Well, I do!" Dickson shouted. "I feel SO different! I feel super strong and super powerful! And I have something else to tell you too. Wait till you hear it!"

But as much as they tried to make him tell, he kept

his secret to himself, giddy and dancing all the way to Arborvine.

Wilma opened the door.

"Well, there're my friends," she said. "Do you want the good news first or the bad news?"

They looked at each other.

"Okay, I'll pick," said Wilma. "The bad news is you all have to go see Mrs. Sloat in her office right away."

"But she thinks I'm at after-school business camp," said Dickson weakly. His superpower voice had vaporized.

"Tell her you got out early. Tell her your company went bankrupt or something. But she said to send you up as soon as I saw you. So, go go go."

"What's the good news?" asked Marwa, forever hopeful.

"Well, honey, I'll think of some by the time you get back," said Wilma.

✳

Dickson's mother, Melinda Sloat, CEO of Happy Valley Village, had her office behind a glass wall right off the atrium at the main entrance. She was standing in her office doorway when she saw them.

"Move these cornstalks somewhere else!" she snapped at her assistants. "My office door looks like a barnyard!"

Halloween decorations had been showing up in the dining rooms and on doorways for a couple of weeks, but now the big stuff was coming into the atrium to get ready for the Halloween party.

"Come in. Sit, please," she said to the three of them. Her voice was cool and prickly. "Dickson, pull up another chair, would you?"

She perched on the edge of her desk, which was the size of a dining room table.

"Dickson, you're out early today."

He sat up straight in his chair, his hands folded in his lap.

"Uh, the teacher got sick."

"Hmm." She brushed some strands of blond hair back from her face. "Well, I had a call from your school today." She stared at him, letting the words sink in. "Do you know why they called me?"

Dickson was finding interesting things to look at on the wall.

"Dickson?"

"I got in a fight," he mumbled.

"Mmm. I couldn't believe it when they told me you'd hit someone. I didn't know what to say. And you have a day of detention! I was so upset I canceled my afternoon meeting."

Addie was chilled just sitting there. The temperature in the room felt around zero. When the people she knew got mad, they yelled. Tish would slam doors, swear, and pack a suitcase. Granny Lu would stomp, shout, and turn an exercise video on extra loud. Mrs. Sloat was as cold and smooth as an ice rink. Addie wondered why Dickson hadn't turned into a little ice cube by now.

Mrs. Sloat was nowhere near finished yet. She had started out slow, but she was picking up steam. The temperature in the room was going from glacial to equatorial fast.

"What if the other boy had been badly hurt? The last thing we need is to have some family sue us or have my name in the papers! What about the reputation of Happy Valley Village? Did you stop to think of that?" She glared at Dickson. Then she started to pace back and forth to and from the window.

"I assured your principal I would look into it and get back to her. Maybe it wasn't your fault. Maybe we could say the other boy did something and we could blame it on him?" She came and stood over them. "I want to hear the whole story. The whole story! And I want to hear what you two know too," she said, pointing a pearly fingernail at Addie and Marwa.

Dickson thawed enough to talk. He mumbled something about Mr. Norris.

"Mr. Norris!" Mrs. Sloat erupted. "What's he got to do with this? Did he put you up to it? Is he trying to take this whole place down?" A red flush spread over her face. She paused to take hold of herself and breathe. She fixed her hair. "Sorry, sweetheart." She settled on her desk again and homed in on Dickson. "Go on, honey," she said, sweet as syrup. "Tell me everything about Mr. Norris." Her eyes had a glint.

Dickson took a deep breath. He started off again, saying something about his online research.

"Marcus Fox, Mrs. Firillo's nephew, said I was a real computer whiz! I checked out the Worldwide Wrestling Entertainment sites and posted my own questions, but

Mr. Norris doesn't have a clue about WWE, and then we found his suit...."

Addie's breath caught.

"Dickson, stop!" she warned.

"What suit?" asked Mrs. Sloat.

But with his mother's full attention, her sugary smile and her little sounds of encouragement, the last thing Dickson could do was stop. Within seconds, he'd spilled the whole story: the suit, the car, how he punched Lucas with his new superpower—his new superpower! Oh, and the Manhattan Project!

It was hard to tell what Mrs. Sloat thought of Dickson's story. From the multiplying wrinkles across her forehead, she was either awestruck or dumbfounded. Dickson was obviously going with awestruck.

He saved the best for last.

"Wait till you hear what I found out in school today when we had research time in the library." He smiled, beaming in his mother's attention. "I didn't even tell you two about this yet.

"I was checking out some of the superhero forums with the new data we have: the belt with *B* on it, the blue suit and car...and..." Dickson paused to make sure they were ready for it. "Today I found there was a superhero in the 1940s and '50s called BREATHALYZER!" He waited for their reaction.

"Isn't that cool? Huh? Breathalyzer! What do you think??!! Guys?"

Addie was furious at Dickson for telling Mr. Norris's secrets. Even if none of them were true.

"Wait, isn't that the name of a breath mint?" Addie said.

"Breath-a-ly-zer?" Marwa whispered to herself.

Mrs. Sloat rose.

"A Breathalyzer is a breath tester the police use," she said, looking darker and angrier than Addie had thought possible. "Dickson, I thought you were telling me the truth, but I don't know where these ridiculous ideas have come from!" She began to pace around her office, looking more and more combustible with every step. "I'm at a loss, a complete loss! There are no such things as superheroes or superpowers! Really, Dickson!"

Dickson had shriveled to almost nothing.

Mrs. Sloat took a deep breath.

"I am very concerned about the influence Mr. Norris has had on you. In fact, I am beginning to think this is all his fault. I wonder...," she said, looking out the window again.

She whipped around.

"I want you three to wait right here."

She called to her assistant.

"I want to see Wilma. Tell her to bring Mr. Norris's file with her. Also Tish, Brad, and find out who Mr. Norris's doctor is. Call Dr. Barker, too. I want them in my office. NOW!"

CHAPTER 23

Mrs. Sloat waited until they had all assembled in her office. Tish gave Addie a look that said "What's going on?" Wilma tried to keep papers from falling out of several fat files she held. Brad stretched his neck and shoulders. Mrs. Sloat's assistant crept in holding a large paper cup in front of her.

"Thought you'd like a coffee, Mrs. Sloat?"

Mrs. Sloat took a long drink.

"Dr. Barker is on his way," said Mrs. Sloat, closing her office door, "but I don't want to keep you all, so let's get right to it. I have received some alarming information about Mr. Norris." She lasered in on Dickson, Addie, and Marwa. "He has apparently been telling these children he is a superhero!"

"No!" Addie blurted out. "He never did!"

"Dickson," Mrs. Sloat said, cutting Addie off and

standing in front of him. "Tell everyone what you told me. Go on, every bit."

Dickson ground out the story again, his eyes glued to the floor.

Mrs. Sloat kept telling him to speak up and prompting him when he left something out. The way she phrased her questions and comments painted a very dark picture of Mr. Norris.

She nodded when Dickson finished, and she saw the nervous smiles on the adults' faces. "I know, it's CRAZY! But," she said, pointing to each of the adults in turn, "here's the thing. What if he's somehow serious about this nonsense?" Their smiles vanished one by one. "What I want to know from each of you is what you have been seeing when you've been with Mr. Norris. Is there some cognitive impairment, dementia, or delusional issue I'm not aware of?"

Dr. Barker stepped into the office.

"Ah, Alan," she said. "Thank you for coming. Please, take a chair." She closed the door behind him and filled him in on the reason for the meeting. By the end of her story, Dr. Barker sat stiff and mute. His eyes darted from one person to another as if making sure he hadn't entered some alternate universe.

"Wilma," Mrs. Sloat said, "why don't you go first. What have you observed?"

Wilma laid her files on Mrs. Sloat's desk and pointed out one page after another.

"Here are the meds he's taking. There have been one

or two changes in them, and this is the latest report from Dr. Mills. This is the record of his vitals...."

"Yes," said Mrs. Sloat, "but what is your assessment? Is he stable? Competent?"

Wilma looked at her.

"As competent as anyone else at Arborvine."

Mrs. Sloat looked unhappy.

"Tish, what about you?"

Tish shrugged.

"In the beginning he could be grumpy, well, actually, he still is, but we've learned to get along okay, I think." She cocked her head to the side. Mrs. Sloat was waiting. "I guess...if you want to know if I think he's losing it, I'd have to say, not at all. He's as sharp as anyone."

"But what about this blue suit Dickson keeps talking about, and the car?"

Tish squirmed.

"The suit is real," she mumbled. "The car"—she shot a glare at Addie—"I didn't know about that."

Mrs. Sloat frowned.

"Anything else, Tish? Anything at all?"

"No, that's it."

"Brad?"

"Uh, well, I'd say he's not impaired mentally. Physically, he's got great muscle tone. He looks like he used to be some kind of athlete. But he was unsteady on his feet when he first got here, that was a given. He told me he hadn't worked out in years. So it's just been a matter of getting him back on his feet and giving him a routine to follow."

"Nothing else?"

Mrs. Sloat leaned back against her desk.

"Okay, here's what we're going to do," she said. "I will talk to Dr. Mills and have him order a complete evaluation. Every test he can think of. When we have all the data, we'll make a decision. Thank you for meeting today. One word of caution. Absolutely, do you hear me, absolutely no discussion of this topic beyond this room. Understood? Remember the client privacy statement you all signed when you were hired."

Addie, Marwa, and Dickson got up to go.

"You three. Wait outside my door. Alan, can I talk to you for a minute?"

She motioned Dr. Barker over to the window.

Addie stood as close as possible to the door, which they hadn't closed all the way.

Mrs. Sloat tried whispering, but since Dr. Barker's hearing wasn't so good, she had to talk louder than she probably would have liked.

"If only he was diagnosed with dementia or Alzheimer's, I could call in the lawyers and have him committed to the memory care wing. Or, if he truly has some kind of psychosis, I could get rid of him that way. If he has any condition where he can't live on his own, then he has to move out of his house. That's what's in the contract we signed with him when HVV got this place."

Dr. Barker whispered to her. Something about "tests and evaluations."

"But we don't want it to take forever," she said. "This

might be our big chance to get rid of him and start building the new 'Country Villas' on his place."

Dr. Barker whispered something that sounded like "What if he's not crazy?"

Mrs. Sloat stared through the window out into the distance.

"A superhero!" she muttered, shaking her head.

"Of course that's ridiculous," said Dr. Barker. "Children will believe anything."

Mrs. Sloat snapped back to reality when she heard a noise. Her head swiveled around. Dickson was pulling his king-sized candy bar out of his pocket and unwrapping it. Even outside her office, she heard it.

"Dickson, don't eat that!" she said, striding out of her office and snatching it away from him. "You know better. Time for you three to leave, BUT here's the thing. I want you to tell me what you see regarding Mr. Norris. I want to know what the staff and residents are saying. Hear me?

"You especially," she said, pointing at Addie. "Your mother's trial month is almost up, and her file could use some help. If you know what's good for you, and her, you tell me everything you notice about Mr. Norris. Every detail, got it?"

She surveyed the three of them. "And no talking about this meeting today. I mean that! Dickson"—she pulled him aside—"you and I will discuss the school incident later at home. Go sit somewhere and do your homework and meet me back here in an hour to go home."

They couldn't leave fast enough.

The three of them dragged their feet down one basement hallway after another on their way back to Arborvine.

"Dickson, you weasel!" Addie was furious. "Did you have to tell everything? And what's going to happen when Mr. Norris finds out we not only looked at his blue suit but the car too!"

"And all those tests they're going to do on him," said Marwa. She looked ready to cry.

Dickson shuffled along behind them, his head down.

They went the rest of the way in silence until they came to a corner in one of the subbasement hallways. There were voices up ahead. Addie put out a hand to stop them.

It was Tish speaking.

"I didn't want to get in trouble, and I'd never tell the Sloat anything anyway, but remember that time, Wilma, with his walker? He started coughing outside and it blew him and me right off our feet."

"He's strong, I'll say that about him." It was Brad. "You know Mrs. Ruckleshaus, well, she told me she'd seen Mr. Norris lifting the hundred-pound weights when I'd left the gym for a minute. Of course, I thought it was just Mrs. Ruckleshaus. But there was a time in the pool. He wanted to do laps, so I let him in, made sure he had everything he needed, and went back to the gym after he yelled at me to leave him alone. I went to check on him about thirty minutes later. He was drying himself off, but the entire pool room, the walls, even the ceiling, were wet. It looked like there'd been a hurricane in there. I started to say something, but he pushed past me and never said a word."

Wilma spoke up then in a quiet voice Addie had never heard her use before.

"Well, then, I thought I was the crazy one, but I'll tell you something. About a week ago, I was going down the hall doing my evening round when I heard this great windy sound coming from his room. I peeked in and saw him standing at the open window. It was like nothing I'd ever seen in my life! He was taking in these huge breaths. His chest grew and grew as he breathed in, and then when he couldn't gulp another drop, he blew and blew all that air out the window. I could hear the trees rustling outside like there was a storm or something.

"Then he heard me, I guess, because he whipped around, and he was still breathing out one of his great big breaths, and it blew me backward. It blew me right back out of that room into the hall with the door slamming shut in my face. I could feel the wind blowing out from under the door. Then it was quiet as a graveyard. I gave a little knock and opened the door a crack and said, 'Mr. Norris, you okay?' He came and pushed the door closed, saying, 'I'm fine, Wilma, leave me alone.' But to this day, I don't know what was going on in that room."

They must have started walking again, because their voices grew fainter.

Marwa had been hugging herself tight, and her eyes couldn't have gotten any bigger. When the voices were gone, she burst forth in a whisper, bright-eyed and sparkling.

"That's it! His superpower is his breath...his strength! Because he's called Breathalyzer. And he's a SUPERHERO!"

CHAPTER 24

Addie wanted to find Mr. Norris to warn him about the tests Mrs. Sloat and the doctor were ordering. What would happen if his secrets were uncovered? Even if none of it was true, he would cringe at having his private life invaded. A sick, queasy feeling spread through her, but as scared as she was of his reaction, she was more scared of what was in store for him.

But she couldn't find him anywhere on Arborvine. She was about to go check the basement and the gym when she ran into her mother.

"Addie, there you are. Time to go home. I'm done for the day." Tish shook her head. "And what a day, right?"

"Tish, I want to find Mr. Norris."

Her mother's face hardened.

"I think I've had enough of Mr. Norris for one day. I want to go home and hear about what you've been up to.

From what Dickson said, I think we have some catching up to do."

"But let me just check in the basement—"

"Forget Mr. Norris! We're going home, we're having dinner, we're gonna talk." Tish slung her bag over one shoulder and headed for the door. She held it open and waited for Addie.

Ever since Mr. Norris had talked to Tish when she had mentioned moving again, Addie had caught her mother looking at her in a new way. A look halfway between puzzled and amazed. It felt weird. Almost as if Tish was noticing her for the first time. And Addie had caught Tish staring at herself in the bathroom mirror. Not putting on lipstick or eyeliner or anything, just staring. She wished Granny Lu was around to make some sense of it, especially when Tish got out the vacuum one day.

※

The first thing Addie wanted to do the next day after school was find Mr. Norris, even though Tish had told her not to spend so much time with him. Dickson was already at HVV, spending his day of detention there, but when she and Marwa walked into Arborvine, they could tell something had happened.

Instead of the afternoon quiet, there was a worried hum of activity. Mrs. Firillo was front and center.

"Oh, dearie," she said, spotting Marwa. "You are just the person I want to see. Can you take care of Izzy? Maybe take her for a walk?" She bent her head close to them. "It's the most awful thing, but Gene, Mr. Trippling, is terribly sick. The nurses think it could be the flu. He might have to go to the hospital." She shook her head. "I want to peek in and see if there's anything he needs, but Izzy gets on his nerves. Can you take her? You are a darling!" She handed the leash to Marwa.

Dickson was there, staring at Mr. Trippling's door.

"Poor Mr. Trippling," he said when he saw Addie and Marwa. "He hates being sick. I wasn't allowed in his room all day, and I was going to show him a cool virtual tour of the British Museum to cheer him up."

He went off with his head down to keep doing the extra homework he'd been given. Since he'd told his mother everything about Mr. Norris the day before, he'd been in a slump. He knew Addie was mad at him. Marwa wasn't happy either. And then there was his mother. Even having superpowers couldn't make a person happy.

"How's Mr. Trippling, do you know?"

Miss Trotter's soft voice snuck up behind Addie.

"Mrs. Firillo says he might have the flu. That's all I know," said Addie.

"Poor soul," said Miss Trotter. She was holding a vase of chrysanthemums. "Do you think I should take these in to him or leave them with a nurse?"

In the end, she gave them to an aide who was looking after Mr. Trippling.

Miss Trotter came back to where Addie was stowing her backpack in a corner of the lounge.

"Malcolm, Mr. Greenberg, made the most beautiful card for him," she said, looking toward Mr. Trippling's door. "In Italian! It makes me so happy that Malcolm's starting to draw again." She shivered. "Goodness, I hope we don't all get the flu."

"Hey, Miss Trotter, have you seen Mr. Norris anywhere?"

"Mmm, no, I haven't, dear."

As Addie checked up and down the Arborvine hallway for him, she saw Mrs. A, C, and D carrying containers of ice cream.

"Three different flavors for Gene," said Mrs. C, "because we didn't know what he likes."

Before Addie could ask them if they'd seen Mr. Norris, Des came down the hallway with a tray.

He winked at her.

"Mrs. Barker asked me to bring Mr. Trippling some of those special stewed prunes she's heard I make." He chuckled.

Addie smiled.

"Yeah," she said. "And talking about Mr. Norris, have you seen him?"

"Not since lunchtime."

Addie got a frightening thought.

"Wow, I hope he hasn't escaped again!"

"All I can tell you is he didn't look like he was going anywhere at lunch. He was too busy telling me exactly what was wrong with his BLT." Des laughed and headed on down the hall.

At that moment, Addie caught sight of Marcus Fox.

"Addie!" He smiled, a big shining grin full of white teeth. "Afternoon! How are you? Waiting for your mom? I had a little time, and it was such a beautiful day, I thought I'd see if Aunt Patsy wanted to go for a walk."

Addie could see gray clouds blowing in, and the sunlight was fading fast. It wasn't her idea of a beautiful day.

"I think she went in her room, but she's really worried about Mr. Trippling. He's sick, maybe with the flu."

"Oh, bummer! Well, I'll check and see if I can talk her into going anyway. After all, what are the nurses here for, right?" He laughed. "Hey, have you seen Mr. Norris?"

She shook her head.

"Nope, not at all."

"Oh, well. See you later!"

Addie wandered down to Miss Trotter's candy dish. Yay, Halloween candy! Some of the dolls were wearing miniature Halloween costumes. One was a ghost, another looked like Little Red Riding Hood, and one was a miniature witch. She would have told Miss Trotter how great the costumes were, but she could hear the sewing machine whirring away in her room and decided not to interrupt. While she straightened the dolls' tiny trick-or-treat bags, she could hear Marcus Fox and Mrs. Firillo talking in her room.

"I can't possibly today."

"Oh, come on, Aunt Patsy, a little fresh air would do you good!"

"Really, I can't."

"Well, it's too bad. I had some time and thought it would be fun for you. I'm swamped with work for the next few days and don't know when I'll be able to come back. What if we get a nice coffee or tea and some pastry? I'll drive."

"I really don't want to go."

"Half an hour and I'll have you back, ready to go back to your duties."

Mrs. Firillo gave a big sigh.

"All right. If you really want to. Let me get my coat."

"And on the way out, maybe you could introduce me to Mrs. Sloat. I thought she'd be a great resource for learning more about the history of this place."

"Well...we can see if she's in her office, I guess."

Marcus hung out in the hallway, looking pleased with himself, while Mrs. Firillo got ready to go.

He had wandered over to talk to the nurse on duty when Addie heard the elevator at the end of the hall. Mr. Norris rounded the corner and started down the hall. He didn't use a cane anymore and walked easily on his own now.

Addie didn't waste a second. She zipped down the hall, waving a hand to stop him.

"Shh," she said, grabbing his sleeve and turning him around. "Marcus Fox." She motioned behind her.

She led him back to the elevator, where she pushed the basement-level button.

"He's looking for you. He's taking Mrs. Firillo out, but then he'll be back. I think you'd better hang out in the basement for a while."

They got to Mrs. Firillo's storage compartment, where Dickson was scrunched up on the sofa. He glanced up, then curled into a ball over his book.

Mr. Norris grunted.

"It smells in here of those awful things you kids eat."

"Here." Addie dug through the plastic bin. "Here's some of the cookies you liked." She settled herself on the sofa and made room for him in the middle.

Dickson still hadn't said a word, but Addie figured the time had come.

"Dickson," she said. "We need to tell Mr. Norris."

Dickson had sunk as far down into the cushions as he could. She couldn't see his face, but the tips of his ears were flaming red.

She put down her chips and faced Mr. Norris.

"I just want you to know we did NOT mean to get you in trouble." Those eyes of his made her drop her head. "I didn't think it would matter." She swallowed. Mr. Norris was silent, but she could feel his eyes riveted on her.

Addie took a deep breath. "Okay, so here's the thing. We took a really quick peek at the blue costume in your house, and then the garage—"

"WHAT?" barked Mr. Norris, so loud that Dickson and Addie both jumped.

He stood up and towered over them.

"We weren't going to go down into the garage," she said. "I promise! But Fluffy ran down and we had to find her." Addie bowed her head. "We saw part of the blue car. Nothing else. I'm really sorry, Mr. Norris."

He was breathing heavily.

"But then...," Addie started, and stopped. "Dickson didn't mean to say anything, right, Dickson?"

Mr. Norris went kind of gray and pasty all over. About the color of gluey papier-mâché in school.

He looked from one to the other.

"You didn't mean to say WHAT?"

"Go on, Dickson."

In bits and pieces, Dickson coughed it out. Addie had to keep reminding Mr. Norris not to shout, yell, or for heaven's sakes scream, because people, meaning Marcus Fox, might hear him upstairs.

By the end, after pacing around the room and up and down the hallway, picking up furniture, and threatening to throw things, Mr. Norris sat slumped on the sofa, eyes closed. He was still so long, Addie wondered if he might have fallen asleep.

When he finally spoke, it sounded like he'd swallowed a load of rocks.

"You've seen the garage? The car? You've all talked about me…with Mrs. Sloat?"

Addie dipped her head. His voice was squeezed so tight, it hurt just to hear him.

"And they're going to run tests on me?"

Dickson started to gather up his things.

"I've got to go meet my mother." He sounded about as miserable as could be. "I guess 'sorry' won't make much difference, Mr. Norris." He kept his eyes on the floor. "And I guess it's not the right time to ask you to use your superpowers to make Mr. Trippling better…?" He looked up, hopeful, but when he saw that Mr. Norris hadn't budged, his head went down again. "But I'll try to find a way to make it up to you, Mr. Norris. I really will."

Mr. Norris gave a low growl that threatened to turn into a roar, and his eyebrows bristled, but he didn't say a word. Just glared at Dickson.

Dickson skittered out, and they were quiet for a long time.

"I don't want to defend Dickson, because he's an all-time good-for-nothing rat maggot of a slug, but you know his mother," Addie said. "I think when she orders him to tell her something, he can't not."

"Mrs. Sloat, the Queen of the Underworld." Mr. Norris laid his head back and closed his eyes.

"What's wrong with Gene Trippling?" he muttered.

"Flu, they think."

"Hmph. Well, I can't do anything about that."

"Right, of course not. Because you're not a super-hero." Addie paused for a second, but he didn't object. "Don't worry about it. You don't have to pretend. If you were a superhero, you'd be out saving people. What good is a superhero if they can't save someone, right?"

The silence between them suddenly grew deeper.

"Exactly," he said in a low voice. He rubbed his face with his hands. "That is... the million-dollar question."

Addie opened a bag of popcorn and started to eat.

"What was it your grandmother used to say about hopes and dreams?" Mr. Norris had his head back on the sofa, staring at the ceiling.

"Yeah, they're a waste of time. Life is just a cold, wet smack in the kisser."

"That's it. Sounds about right to me."

"Want some popcorn?"

"Thanks, I think I will."

He picked away at the popcorn in his hand.

"What am I going to do?" he said to himself.

She looked at him.

"Don't worry about it. They'll run their stupid tests and find out you're just a normal, old, not-crazy, weird guy...about as far from being a superhero as this piece of popcorn."

"Thanks. That's very reassuring."

CHAPTER 25

"Whoa, what happened to you?"

Addie found Dickson outside the school with dark splotches on his sweatshirt and pants.

"There's more," he said, slowly taking off his hat. His hair was wet and stood up in spikes.

"I tried to wash my hair in the bathroom sink." He leaned his head toward her. "Do you see any pieces of pasta still? Spaghetti pie day has never been my favorite."

"I thought it was okay, but then I didn't have to wear it."

"Ewww!" Marwa came up to them. "What happened?"

Dickson pulled his hat back on.

"I keep telling Dickson to eat at the nut-free table, like you and I do for fifth-grade lunch," Addie said to Marwa. "But he doesn't listen."

"Yeah, it's good," said Marwa. "Addie and me sit

there every day. The other kids at the table are nice. You should do it when fourth grade has lunch."

Dickson grunted.

"Well, I guess we can conclude I don't have any superpowers." Dickson hoisted his backpack and started to trudge toward the path. "I'm a superZERO!"

"Because, as I keep telling you, Mr. Norris is not a superhero!" Addie glared at him.

"Well, I say he is," said Marwa, her nose in the air, "but you know, Dickson, I'm just saying, as a fourth grader it might be better if you didn't wear that hat."

He spun around.

"What's wrong with my hat? It's my new super-duper winter trooper trapper hat! It was the only one in plaid with white fur. My mom got it for me for..." He didn't finish the sentence. So Addie did it for him.

"For telling everything on Mr. Norris.... Am I right?" She was disgusted.

Dickson turned and walked on in silence.

"Hey, guess who I saw in the hallway today." Addie caught up to him. "Marshall, that's who. He said you told him at lunch all about this old superhero you know called Breathalyzer. He thought it was funny, but then he kind of wanted to know if it was true. You must have been pretty convincing."

"Well, he had me under the table! What was I supposed to do?" Dickson kept his head down. "Anyway, what do you know? You don't have to eat lunch with those kids every day. At first they didn't believe me, but I told them about what's been happening at HVV."

Addie rolled her eyes.

"Dickson...really?"

"Man, when they started to believe me, Lucas got paper towels and helped wipe me off, Marshall gave me his Fruit Roll-Up, and the others sat with me at the lunch table and wanted to know more about what Mr. Norris is really like. It was pretty amazing."

"Yeah, and it's going to be great when they show up at HVV. I tried to tell them it was some crazy story of yours." Addie was fed up with him. "But I don't know if they believed me or not. Dickson, you better tell them you made it up."

Dickson, at that point, decided to take off and run down the path, his backpack bumping and bouncing, his plaid trapper hat flapping.

"Too bad he doesn't have superpowers." Marwa sighed. "He could use some."

※

Minerva was waiting for Addie in her room. They had gotten to the part in *The Wind in the Willows* where Toad is dumped out of his caravan into the dusty road after a car sideswipes it. At first, Addie thought it was kind of stupid to be reading about a rat and a mole who spend all their time rowing on a river. But the more she read with Minerva, the more she got into it. There were lots of funny parts, and drawings, and she could follow the adventures on the map at the front of the book.

"Hello, Adelaide." Minerva got up from her chair

and began to gather a few things together. "I was waiting for you. The library needs someone to sit at the desk for a couple of hours and I said I'd do it. All right if we read there?"

Addie left her backpack, said hello to the bird, and they took off. The library was on the lower level of the main building, so they took two different elevators and several long halls to get there.

Minerva swerved through the library door on her scooter, unpacked the bag of books she was returning, and took her place behind the desk.

"Okay, Adelaide. All yours. Ruby goes outside in that parking area."

They had agreed that whenever they went somewhere, Addie could park Ruby the red scooter. She got on the seat, took an extra spin up and down the hall because it was so much fun, and backed Ruby (beeping all the way) into a space.

She pulled up a chair next to the desk and opened *The Wind in the Willows*.

"Before we start," said Minerva, looking around, "since there's no one here, I have some information for you."

She dug through her large canvas bag on the floor.

"Did I tell you Gene asked me to look into Marcus Fox? He's had concerns about him, and he knew I'd done research for academic papers I had to write at my university.... Oh, where is it?" She was sinking deeper and deeper into her canvas bag. If she went too far in, Addie was afraid she'd have to pull her out.

Minerva resurfaced, a bit flushed and out of breath.

"Got it! Anyway, I can handle a limited amount of online research, and what I can't manage, my friends at the university library can."

She laid a pile of papers on the desk.

"Okay, here we go." She thumbed through the papers.

"Hello, Minerva!"

A woman with white hair and a bright red sweater pushed a wheeled shopping cart up to the desk. It was decorated with a garland of pumpkins and fall leaves.

"Mary, good afternoon," said Minerva. "Do you know Adelaide?"

They chatted about the books the woman was returning.

"Adored this one! That one, oh my goodness, too dark and violent! Nearly gave me a heart attack!"

While Addie waited to hear about Marcus Fox, they talked on and on until the woman ended up with one mystery ("not too scary," "set in southern France," said Minerva) and a biography of a queen who had been dead for five hundred years ("perfect!" said Mary).

"Now, where were we?" Minerva heaved a sigh when the woman had gone. She dug through the papers on her desk again. "I'm looking for a picture...anyway, for one thing, I have a suspicion Marcus Fox isn't related to Patsy Firillo at all. I could be wrong, but anybody could tell her they're related, and half the time she wouldn't know the difference. Also, and I'm certain of this, Marcus Fox doesn't work at the newspaper."

"Wow, really?"

"Not at all. In fact, he is associated with a group that employed his grandfather. Here's the picture I was looking for. This is a photo of his grandfather."

Addie looked at the grainy black-and-white photo.

"That man there is Marcus Fox's grandfather, Sergei Marzukhov."

"Same big smile," said Addie.

"He's probably smiling because it's an award ceremony for a breakthrough in atomic radiation research. See the date?"

Addie looked closely.

"1948."

"See the man next to him? Guess who that is?"

Addie read the caption. The name Norris jumped out at her. She looked at Minerva.

"That's Mr. Norris's father. He had been working for the Manhattan Project years earlier but had suddenly left that job. No reason was given. I wonder if he was fired."

"Marcus Fox mentioned the Manhattan Project."

Minerva eyed her.

"Did he? At any rate, Mr. Norris's father set up a research lab in California with Mr. Marzukhov as his assistant. They worked there until they won this award in 1948, and then there was an accident. There was a clipping from our local paper in November of 1948 saying the Norris family had returned home. I found an obituary for the elder Mr. Norris a month later, but strangely, no cause of death was given."

Minerva looked down at the photo again. "It seems, shortly after both men won the award when this picture was taken, Mr. Marzukhov stopped working for Mr. Norris's father and started his own research laboratory. That's the company Marcus Fox is apparently involved with. It's called Obsidian Enterprises now, but it's had several different names in the past."

"What do they do?" asked Addie.

"Well, they were mentioned here and there, but their online presence is practically invisible." She looked at Addie. There was a glint in her eyes. "However, my friends at the university did some real digging."

"Yeah?"

"Obsidian has ties to research in various fields of extreme science... questionable science, I might call it... most notably in the area of weapons manufacturing."

"That doesn't sound good. And that's what Marcus Fox does?"

"I'm not exactly clear on what his role is, but yes, he seems to work for or with them." She pulled out another paper. "Here's another item my friends came across in a 1948 newspaper in California. It mentions a fire at Mr. Norris's lab. It says the fire was quickly extinguished and only one assistant, Mr. Norris's son, sustained minor injuries. So it sounds as if they were working together on some experiment when the accident happened."

"Does it say anything about what kind of injuries Mr. Norris, our Mr. Norris, had?"

"No, it only said minor injuries." Minerva looked at

her notes. "I figured he must have been about sixteen then."

Addie smiled to herself.

"Huh, so maybe instead of being a superhero, he's a mad scientist!"

There was a moment of total silence before Minerva turned to stare at her.

"What did you say?"

CHAPTER
26

"Hurry up!" Dickson motioned to Addie and Marwa outside of school. "Don't you want to find out what happened?"

Mrs. Sloat had told him she was having an important meeting that day. She was so excited about it she told Dickson to skip FEEBOL and come back right after school. If, as she hoped, the meeting went well, they would go straight home and celebrate. Dickson was hoping for pizza.

Earlier that day, he'd found Addie and Marwa in the hallway at snack time. He was trying to talk to them as they lined up for the vegetable trolley put out by the cafeteria but it was difficult with his new admirers.

"Come on, Dickson, tell us what he's really like!" said Marshall. "What's he said?"

"Do you still have the handkerchief he gave you?"

said Lucas, who still had a bit of a black eye. "Can you bring it to school?"

Dickson managed to pull Addie and Marwa aside when Marshall and Lucas started to go for each other with the squirt bottles of ranch dressing.

"Who do you think my mom has a meeting with today?" He was wriggling while he waited for them to guess.

When they both shrugged, Dickson let out, "Marcus Fox!" in a strangled whisper.

Addie paused with a carrot stick in her mouth.

"He's coming to see your mother? About what?"

"Not only him, but some people he works with."

"The newspaper people?" said Marwa.

"No," said Addie, thinking, "it might be the people Minerva told me about. The company that does research and makes weapons. Obsidian. Minerva said he doesn't work for the newspaper, remember? I wonder what he wants with your mother?"

When they got to HVV after school, Dickson talked them into going straight to his mother's office to see what had happened, but they didn't get that far. Mrs. Sloat was outside the main entrance shaking hands and saying goodbye to a group of men, all wearing dark suits, white shirts, and dark ties. Except for Marcus Fox. He, at least, wore a brightly striped tie.

"Hi, kids!" He smiled and waved at them before hopping into a black SUV. There were, in fact, three black SUVs pulled up at the curb. They pulled off slowly in a convoy.

"I don't care what you think of him." Marwa sighed. "You have to admit he's good-looking."

Mrs. Sloat sighed too as she looked after the cars.

"They are going to help me put Happy Valley Village on the map," she said in a dreamy voice.

Normally, Addie would think being on a map was a good idea, but coming from Mrs. Sloat, this didn't sound good at all.

They followed Mrs. Sloat indoors, where work was underway bringing in even more decorations for the upcoming Halloween party in the atrium. Custodians and the landscape crew were everywhere: on ladders pulling up strings of tiny lights, bringing in wagons of pumpkins and chrysanthemums. Aunt Tina's brother Matt was wheeling in a couple of hay bales with a scarecrow slumped on top, but he managed a wave to Addie.

"Mrs. Sloat," called her assistant, "another parent calling for you."

Mrs. Sloat seemed to remember there were children following her. She turned.

"Do you know anything about the phone calls I've been getting today from parents of students at your school? They are asking me what in heaven's name I know about rumors of a superhero here." She zeroed in on Dickson. "Somehow, word is getting around."

The assistant called to her again.

"I'm coming." She clicked off across the polished floor on her high heels.

The three of them watched the decorating going on.

Then there was the Halloween candy dish at the main desk to investigate.

Before they had finished choosing, Mrs. Sloat was back in front of them.

"Leave that candy for the residents, please. You, there, up on the ladder." She called to one of the custodians. "I want some strings of lights hanging straight down where the ceiling is highest. On the sides there, they can be looped. Now," she said, turning to Dickson. "I've got one more thing I need to take care of." She looked at Addie.

"Is your mother with Mr. Norris today?"

"I don't know, she didn't tell me."

"All right, well, I need to see him." She stared off and shook her head. "Why is everyone so interested in that man?" She took a deep breath. "Dickson, find something to do. I'll be free in about half an hour. Then we'll go home." She clamped a hand on top of his head and shook it. "To celebrate!"

Arborvine was quieter than the day Mr. Trippling was so sick. The nurse on duty said his medication had kicked in and his fever was gone. She didn't expect him to be going to the hospital. In fact, they now thought he'd caught a cold, not the flu.

"Can I see him?" asked Dickson.

"Better not, honey, we don't want you catching whatever it is. But I'll tell him you were asking about him, okay?"

They picked out candies from Miss Trotter's dish.

All the dolls and stuffed animals were wearing costumes now. In fact, most of the doorways had some kind of Halloween or fall decoration. Mr. Greenberg had a HAPPY HALLOWEEN sign. It looked like it was hand-painted, and Addie wondered if he'd done it himself. Mrs. Firillo was fixing a fall flower arrangement in the lounge; Minerva had hung up a paper witch riding a broomstick. Everyone had something except for Mr. Norris, of course.

"Superheroes don't have time for Halloween decorations," said Marwa in her most serious voice.

"I want to warn him Mrs. Sloat is coming to see him," said Addie. She listened at his closed door. "It doesn't sound like he's there."

She knocked softly on his door but got no answer.

Mrs. Firillo called to them to give her an opinion on the arrangement.

"Is it lopsided? I could add more greens...." Something down the hall caught her attention. "Uh-oh, I can finish this later."

Coffee in hand, Mrs. Sloat, closely followed by Babs Duckworthy, was bearing down on them.

Mrs. Firillo grabbed Marwa's hand.

"I think this is a good time to take Izzy for a walk, dearie."

"Can I come too?" said Dickson.

Marwa got Izzy and she, Mrs. Firillo, and Dickson scooted out the door just in time.

"Not now, Babs," Mrs. Sloat was saying, "I have to meet with him alone."

She went straight down the hall to Mr. Norris's door

and knocked loudly. Without waiting for an answer, she opened his door and walked in.

"Mr. Norris? Are you awake? We need to have a chat."

Addie stared at the door as it shut firmly. She swore to herself, wishing she'd gone into his room and warned him.

"Darn it," said Babs Duckworthy to herself, "when am I ever going to get my story on him for the newsletter?"

She looked at Addie. "What do you know about Mr. Norris? Does your mother tell you things about him? I've been hearing rumors." She glanced over her shoulder. "I heard the local press called Mrs. Sloat about him. And some residents told me there were children stopping them on their walks asking about him!"

"Well, I don't know about that," said Addie. "But I can tell you something..." She lowered her voice. She glanced over her shoulder just the way Mrs. Duckworthy had. "Did you know about the big meeting Mrs. Sloat had today with Marcus Fox? You know he's the nephew of Mrs. Firillo? At least, he SAYS he's her nephew."

Babs Duckworthy's eyes opened wider and wider behind her glasses.

"You say that happened today?"

Addie nodded, dead serious.

"Mmm-hmm. They just left. Three large black SUVs. If I were you I'd find out what you can about Obsidian Enterprises....I don't know, but I think Mrs. Sloat is up to something. If you know what I mean."

By this point, Mrs. Duckworthy was somewhere between horrified and elated.

"Sounds like a juicy story! Do you know anything more?"

While they were talking, the voices behind Mr. Norris's closed door had been getting louder and louder. Addie wished she could get closer to hear, but now that she'd hooked Mrs. Duckworthy, there was no losing her.

Even so, she caught a word or two.

"PERFECTLY CAPABLE NOW!" (Mr. Norris)... "TESTS!" (Mrs. Sloat)... "NO TESTS!" (Mr. Norris)... "RUMORS...PHONE CALLS...ULTIMATUM!" (Mrs. Sloat)...and a fearsome avalanche of swearing (Mr. Norris).

Suddenly, there was a period of profound silence out of which grew a sound Addie had never heard before. It wasn't words, it wasn't voices, it was more like the ocean slipping back from the shore before rising up into a great wave. Then came the crash of an explosion.

After that, all was quiet. Residents peeked out of their doors. The nurse ran down the hall to Mr. Norris's room.

Babs Duckworthy realized she was gripping Addie's arm.

"Heavens, what was that?"

She hurried off to be the first to find out.

Within minutes, there was Brad loping down the hall, then an EMT team with a stretcher, then more nurses, and finally Dr. Barker.

Mrs. Sloat was carried down the hall on the stretcher, holding an ice pack to her head and stammering.

"Alan, that man..." She was clutching Dr. Barker's

sleeve, pulling him along with her. "He's irrational....I fell....No, I was blown...then...and then...He's crazy!"

As she passed by Addie on the stretcher, she looked so wild and shaken, Addie almost felt sorry for her.

Once the EMTs, nurses, staff, and residents had gone, Addie crept down the hall.

She peeked around Mr. Norris's doorway. There was only one nurse with him. He sat on his bed while she finished up checking his temperature and blood pressure.

"How are you feeling now, Mr. Norris?" The nurse said it loudly as if he was hard of hearing.

"I keep telling you I'm fine! It was just some kind of spell. I get them every now and then."

"Well, I'll check on you regularly to be sure, and I've put in a call to Dr. Mills. He might want to see you and look at your meds. Can I get you anything right now? How about someone to pick up your room?"

That was when the rest of the room came into focus. It looked like a hurricane had whipped through. Lamps were knocked over, clothes and books were splayed on top of each other, newspapers and magazines papered the floor.

"I'll do it," he said.

The nurse started to say something.

"It's all right," said Addie, speaking up. "I can help."

The nurse looked at Addie and then at Mr. Norris. He nodded.

After the nurse left, Mr. Norris closed his eyes and let out a long, slow breath. A mixture of annoyance and disgust.

Addie went closer, stepping over books, a towel, several shoes.

"What happened?"

Mr. Norris looked grim.

"I sneezed."

"Huh?"

Addie took another look around the room.

"What do you mean you sneezed?"

He opened his eyes.

"This is why I try not to sneeze very often." Then his face wrinkled up. "At least, if it had to happen to somebody, it was the Sloat." If it had been the beginning of a smile wrinkling his face, it suddenly vanished. "Now she's really going to go for me."

Addie sat down in the one chair left upright.

"You better have the whole picture then," she said. "How about I get one of the aides to make you some tea or something before I tell you?"

"Oh, spit it out, for heaven's sakes. It can't get much worse."

"Okay, but don't get mad at me. I'm just trying to help."

"For Pete's sake, get on with it!"

"So, I need to tell you what Minerva found out about Marcus Fox, and then I need to tell you about the meeting Mrs. Sloat had this afternoon...."

CHAPTER 27

Addie and Tish were having a late dinner in their apartment when Tish's cell phone rang. Tish listened, looked at Addie, and when the call ended, said, "Mr. Norris has disappeared. They can't find him anywhere."

She reached her hand across the table and laid it on Addie's arm.

"You're thinking what I'm thinking, right? We should go."

"Yeah," said Addie, getting her jacket. "We should go."

She'd been worried ever since the episode of the Sneeze and telling Mr. Norris about Marcus Fox and Mrs. Sloat earlier in the afternoon. He'd looked terrible when she'd left him at dinnertime. Wilma had promised to keep an eye on him. But that wouldn't help the trouble he was in.

As she and Tish grabbed hats and coats for the windy night, she couldn't figure out why this felt oddly familiar.

Then, of course, she knew. Whenever Tish got in trouble, she'd take off. Disappear. Maybe just for a night. Maybe two. Once it was a week.

Granny Lu would stomp, grit her teeth, complain to her customers, and watch exercise videos. Then keep on going as if nothing had happened. Tish would show up and Granny Lu would sigh and welcome her back.

Addie could feel her mother walking beside her in the dark. Tish seemed more settled recently, like maybe there was no storm brewing. But then, you could never be sure of what was just over the horizon.

"You know what?" Tish said, stopping. "We should check his house."

"And the garage," said Addie.

Tish looked at her.

"Right."

But he was not in either of those places, so they hurried on to Arborvine.

Addie left Tish checking in with the Arborvine staff. Wilma, Brad, and the nurses were huddled together talking about a change the doctor had made to Mr. Norris's medication that afternoon after the Sneeze took place. Mrs. Firillo, in a flowered robe, was holding Izzy outside Mr. Trippling's door. Mrs. A, C, and D were sitting in front of the TV without watching it. Minerva was talking to Miss Trotter as she wheeled Mr. Greenberg back to his room.

There was enough going on that no one noticed Addie going down the hall. She hadn't said anything to

Tish, but she knew exactly where she would look for Mr. Norris.

It was dark outside, and she didn't have a flashlight, but as she had hoped, the padlock to the tower door, once she found it hidden in the ivy, hadn't been fixed and was still unlocked. Before she went in, she looked up to the top of the tower. Her hair kept blowing in front of her face. It was too dark to see if anything, or anyone, was up there.

It was even windier at the top of the tower. Someone had said this was the tail end of a hurricane. She could hear it blowing before she pushed the door open. When she did get it open, at first she saw nothing, but then, there he was leaning over the stone wall.

He heard the door scraping across the floor, because he turned at once. The wind suddenly died down and it was quiet.

"Oh, it's you," he said, turning back. "You're interrupting my solitude." He was partly propped, partly collapsed over the wall.

"Well, you interrupted my dinner," Addie said.

"Please, don't let me keep you. I didn't invite you up here." He was mumbling, and even though the air was still, it was hard to understand him.

"Thought I'd come see how much more trouble you were getting yourself into."

"As if it's my fault!" He tried to swing himself around to face her but only ended up losing his balance and falling down. He seemed to be having a hard time sitting up—he kept listing to one side, until she sat down beside him and shoved him upright.

"What's the matter with you? Why can't you sit up? You're not getting Mr. Trippling's cold, are you?"

"Oh, who knows? They keep changing my medications. Think my sneeze with Mrs. Sloat alarmed them. And they watch me while I swallow the stupid pills."

"Hey." She nudged him. "Are we staying up here all night? We're out of the wind, but this stone floor is pretty cold on my butt." He was slumped against her. She couldn't tell if he was awake or not.

"Girls shouldn't use words like 'butt,'" he mumbled. "And that was no wind. That was me."

He was drifting off again.

She elbowed him, "Say that again?"

He gave a chuckle that turned into a cough.

"Practicing...have to tell your friend Marwa about my sneeze. Or Mrs. Sloat can." A wheezy laugh caught in his throat. "Couldn't sneeze like that a few weeks ago. Can't get a cold, though." He shuddered. "Sneezing and coughing...means trouble."

"Mrs. Sloat is going to have it in for you now." Addie didn't even want to think about what that would look like. "So you're still sticking to your story that it was just a sneeze? Come on. What really happened in there?"

A grumble came from deep in his chest.

"She is...a...can't use language like that in front of a girl."

"You think I haven't heard those words? So what's she gone and done now?"

"She's got me." He spat out each word in a fury. "Either way. She's got the doctor ordering tests. If I have dementia, you know, losing my marbles, she'll lock me up in prison, or what she calls the 'memory care wing,' and take the rest of my property. It's in the stupid contract I signed years ago…and if I'm not crazy but if the doctors find I have, you know…any unusual abilities, she will threaten to expose me. Either way, it's the end."

"You forgot another possibility. What if you're not crazy and you don't have any of those abilities you said. Like, what if you're just a normal old geezer?"

He thought about it.

"Easier said than done. I don't trust her for a minute. She won't give up till she finds something wrong with me."

He pulled his coat around himself and growled.

"I'd bet you anything it's that Marcus Fox and his bunch you were telling me about, who want my father's papers, his notes from his experiments. Of course, the Sloat's thrilled…said they'd pay for new buildings to be built where my house and garage are."

"Why does Marcus Fox care so much about the papers?"

He let his head fall back against the wall. He was silent for so long she thought he was asleep.

"Come on." She nudged him. "What is it?"

"I should have gotten rid of them years ago…very sensitive…could be dangerous if they got into the wrong hands." His head fell so far forward she could barely hear him. "I never wanted it. Never wanted any of it. Or asked for it. Tired of the whole blasted mess."

He leaned his head in her direction.

"Remember when you said…what good is a superhero if they can't save people? Well, what if a person isn't a superhero but more of a freak?"

CHAPTER 28

Mr. Norris was falling asleep and not making any sense.

"Come on," said Addie. "I'm cold and you must be too. Let's go."

"No, no, no, no...I'm going to spend the night up here...like I used to."

"Oh, no, you're not. Come on."

Addie stood, grabbed one of his arms and tried to pull him up. She couldn't even lift him an inch. Man, he weighed a ton. How was she ever going to get him back to Arborvine? She remembered a few rocky nights when Granny Lu had to get Tish into bed. It had been one step at a time.

She took a deep breath, looked down at the slumped mound of Mr. Norris, and gave him a good kick.

"Ow!"

"Come on, get up," she said with a yank.

She pulled and kicked some more. The disassembled

pieces of Mr. Norris began to connect and work their way upward.

"Wait a minute...not feeling too well...one more breath of fresh air."

He steadied himself against the wall and started to inhale. Addie waited. She could hear him pulling air in. It sounded like wind. Or maybe it *was* the wind. Addie got impatient. He was taking forever. Then a breezy sound kicked in as he exhaled. Slowly at first, then picking up in strength and force. It wasn't loud, but it was powerful. It was the wind after all, she realized, because she could see the tree branches moving back and forth.

"Enough fresh air," she said. "Let's go."

Propping him up on one side, Addie pulled him toward the door step by step. He didn't have his cane, so she was the only thing keeping him from falling.

"You know," he said as Addie maneuvered him through the doorway, "at one time, I used to be able to jump off this tower and blow so I'd float down to the ground."

"Yeah, sure."

"And I was working on the power to blow and erase people's memories..."

Addie had him at the top of the stairs. It was a long, steep, treacherous way down, and he was getting heavier by the minute.

"Look, you'd better sit and go down on your butt."

"What did I say about that word? Hey!" He complained as Addie pushed him down to sit. "Watch it!"

"Okay, now slide down each step."

She coaxed and pushed and pulled. Step by step. It

was going to take years. And Mr. Norris was getting sleepier and starting to hallucinate.

"You know, I remember that night as if it was yesterday. The night of the accident. Father could never be sure...if it was really an accident or not. He was so careful...about everything. He had suspicions. He'd fired his lab assistant and then...the experiment. I was there because Father needed me to help. But it went wrong.... The core slipped, it went over the threshold, the point of no return....There was a flash of blue light...too much radiation exposure. That's when it changed me....Father got too much. That's why he died. You remember Father, don't you?"

"Uh-huh." Addie nodded. "Move your foot out of the way."

"He always hoped I'd be a scientist like him. And Mother..." Mr. Norris sighed. "She wanted me to be a hero and save the world. Ha! Every mother's dream, right?" He sounded bitter.

"Whoa, come back here!" Addie caught him as he started to fall over to one side.

"I could take a little nap...."

"Not yet. Wait till you're back in your bed."

She whacked him on his back.

"Come on, Mr. Norris, wake up! Keep coming down the steps."

"I'm tired...always having to be someone else. Never wanted to have a mission...save people." He shivered. "That accident on the highway was the worst. The high-speed chase. Standing in the middle of the highway.

Blowing the convict's car back...back until he and the police...all piled up, crashing into each other."

He wasn't making any sense at all, and Addie was paying attention to only half of what he said, but at least his stories were keeping him awake and she could guide him down the steps.

"Then there was the fire...you know what happens if you blow on a fire? That was a big mistake. Especially for the neighboring buildings. And the bank robbery... oh, boy...when I sucked all the air out of the bank, oxygen too...everyone, robbers, tellers, customers, guards, everyone passed out...almost died."

"We're getting there. Keep moving."

"The Guild wanted me to try flying. I could lift myself up off the ground and move forward by pinpointing my breath, but what happens when you're hundreds of feet off the ground and you need to take a breath? Or you have to cough?"

"Hey, we made it!"

They were at the bottom of the stairs. Addie pulled him up to stand and they went through the door to the outside.

She'd been working so hard, it felt good to stand for a moment in the cool evening air.

Mr. Norris shifted his weight against her, turned around to look back, and blew.

The door slammed shut behind them.

"Was that...?"

But she couldn't wait for an answer. Voices were coming from the far end of the main building. Addie saw flashlights waving back and forth.

"I think they're out looking for you, Mr. Norris. Do you want to be found?"

"No! Please, get me back to my own bed."

"Okay, then hurry up and we'll go in this door before they see us."

He shuffled as fast as he could to the door.

Once inside, Addie looked up and down the long, deserted hallway. They were in a section where residents had their own apartments. Each resident put some of their own furniture outside their door. One apartment had a side table with fake flowers and family photographs. Another had a bench with a map of Texas above it. In one alcove, there was a whole dining room table with chairs and unused place settings. No one was around. It was like some weird ghost town.

Mr. Norris was leaning so heavily on her, she thought she'd have to sit him down to rest in every chair they passed. Until she saw the scooter. It was shiny blue and parked outside a door.

She peered at the name on the door.

"Well, thank you, Mrs. Harold Kleinstuber, for leaving your key in the scooter. I promise I'll bring it back." She dragged Mr. Norris over and plopped him on the seat. "Keep your feet in. I'm going to stand in front of you."

By swiveling the seat, Mr. Norris could be slumped mostly sideways on the scooter while Addie stood in front of him by the handlebars. It would be a miracle, she thought, if he didn't fall off.

The scooter came to life and they whirred in slow motion down the hall. Mr. Norris was falling asleep again and, every time they went around a corner, was in danger of sliding off.

She jabbed him.

"Mr. Norris, wake up! Keep talking about whatever it was. The weird accident or flying or whatever."

"Mmm, I wasn't cut out for any of it...always trying to be someone else. Someone they wanted me to be. I was so scared...all the time. Let me tell you, trying to save people all day long will do it to you. So I stayed away from everyone for years and hid. Spent time in Mexico, Norway, Australia." He cleared his throat. "As I'm sure your teachers would say, I didn't live up to my full potential."

His head drooped forward.

Addie needed more help if they were ever going to make it back to Arborvine. That was when she spotted it. Stopping the scooter at the next apartment door, she dug through a bowl of Halloween candy on a table until she found the hottest, spiciest candies in the bunch.

"Here," she said, pushing one into his mouth.

She watched him fumble, getting his first taste of hot cinnamon.

He woke up, swore a blue streak, and spat it out all at once.

"Trying to poison me!"

He slumped back in the seat, but at least he was halfway awake.

"Okay, we're going. Try to sit up."

It was easier said than done. He was like a lump of something that had sprung a leak and deflated. His long gray hair looked as if it hadn't met a brush in months.

His tweed jacket must have been handed down to him from some prehistoric relative. Give him a shopping cart of cans, bottles, and old plastic bags and he'd look like a homeless person. How could anyone ever think this guy was a superhero?

"You'll feel better in the morning, Mr. Norris. This is going to seem like some weird dream. You'll forget all these crazy stories you're telling."

Addie backed the scooter into one of the elevators.

"Where are we?" Mr. Norris asked.

"Almost back at Arborvine."

Addie thought of how everybody would be upset with Mr. Norris when they saw him, pestering him with questions, demanding to know where he'd been, why he'd wandered off. If Mrs. Sloat saw him acting crazy and delirious, she would have clear evidence for taking his property.

"You know, what you need is a plan." She thought of maps, how they could be simple or complicated but were always reassuring. They showed the way.

She looked down at Mr. Norris slumped in his seat. He wasn't normally crazy like this, but Mrs. Sloat sure wanted to believe he was nuts. So what if…

When they were out of the elevator in the next empty hall, she jolted him awake by feeding him two extra-strong peppermints.

"Mr. Norris, I've thought of something!"

She crouched down in front of him.

"I know how you can get rid of Mrs. Sloat and Marcus Fox and all of them!"

Through a cloud of peppermint, he blinked and tried to focus on her.

She told him her plan.

When she'd finished, he stared at her, a thundering frown spreading across his face.

"I don't think it will work," he grumbled.

"But think about it. Mrs. Sloat would leave you alone, so would any silly superhero nuts, and Marcus Fox and his company....It's the only way."

He was quiet for a long time, refusing any more candy. But he was wide awake.

"Do you really think it would work?"

Addie put her hand out to shake his.

"I will make it work," she said.

He looked at her hand, then at her, with those dark, deep eyes that had first fixed on her in Mrs. Firillo's storage compartment. They weren't as fierce or angry now. They were lined with red and sagged with bleary tears.

He took her hand. They shook on it.

"Take me to Arborvine, then," he said. "I feel like I'm going to my death."

Addie rolled her eyes.

"I know it'll be hard, but don't be such a drama queen!"

They whirred into the last elevator.

"How did you come to be so smart about people?" asked Mr. Norris. "I never was."

"You learn a lot when you hang around Lulu's House of Hair."

CHAPTER 29

It had been the busiest Halloween ever and it was only lunchtime.

The night before, when Addie got Mr. Norris back to Arborvine, there had been a general uproar when he was found...and about the condition he was found in. After he collapsed on his bed, it took a while to locate a doctor on a Friday night. When one finally came and did his best to check Mr. Norris over while he was sound asleep, he said Mr. Norris was fine (exactly what the nurses had been telling him) but his medications probably needed adjusting, and what he most needed was a good night's sleep.

Before he left, however, the doctor leafed through Mr. Norris's medical file.

"I see a couple of reports from HVV doctors," Addie heard him say to the nurses, "but I don't recognize any of these other names. And most seem to be from foreign countries."

"Oh, he told me once," said Addie, quickly jumping in, "he lived in a lot of other countries." At least that part was true. "And he liked getting different opinions, so he went to a different doctor every time." Mr. Norris had told her on their long scooter journey how he'd forged doctors' signatures for years because he didn't want anyone discovering what a freak he was. Another one of his crazy, rambling stories.

Once the excitement had died down on Arborvine, Addie found Minerva and asked her if they could send an emergency email.

Minerva raised her eyebrows, made sure Addie was all right, and nodded.

Addie sent a prayer up into the universe that Dickson would check his email at home. In the message, she gave him a brief rundown of what had happened but didn't dare say what her plan was in case his mother saw it. Since he had a major part to play, she told him to call her as soon as possible on Tish's cell phone.

She turned to Minerva.

"I need to call Marwa before it's too late, but...but... I'm going to need your help." Addie's eyes filled up. She didn't know why. It was really annoying. She brushed the tears away.

Minerva looked directly at her.

"I think you've had a lot going on lately, am I right? As long as no one will get hurt...what do you need?"

And then the whole story and her plan came tumbling out.

When Addie finished, Minerva raised her eyebrows.

"Clever, Adelaide. I knew you would turn out to be an interesting person."

⁕

The next morning, Saturday, Addie got to Arborvine so early the night shift nurses and aides were still on duty. She talked to the residents who were early risers and explained what she was asking them to do. The night before, Minerva had talked to the ones who stayed up late.

Marwa's mother, Mrs. Omar, was due to start work at 8 a.m., so the two of them came together.

Addie saw Marwa come running down the hall.

"This is so exciting!"

For the first time ever that Addie knew of, Marwa was not wearing a skirt or dress.

Marwa saw Addie's look.

"Hey, you said there was a lot of work to do. Well, I am ready to do work!" She wore jean overalls, a jean jacket, and leather ankle boots. And her flower head-band. "And everything we need to work with, see?" She held up a box of trash bags and a pair of work gloves.

Addie nodded.

"Awesome."

Mrs. Omar caught up to them. She was smiling but her eyes looked worried. She said something in Arabic to Marwa.

Marwa nodded and turned to Addie.

"You know last night when we talked on the phone, I told my mother what you and your mother were saying.

My mother didn't understand and almost didn't let me come, but your mother did a good job talking to her and I said it in Arabic to her. She thinks we're just working to get ready for the Halloween party. So she said okay even though Halloween is a very new thing."

Addie said to Mrs. Omar, "Thanks for letting Marwa come today to help."

"Thank you," said Mrs. Omar, and patted Addie on the shoulder. She said something to Marwa in Arabic.

"She says is it really okay if I spend the night with you tonight? She's a little worried even after your mother talked to her about it on the phone."

Addie said, yes, right away. "Don't worry, Mrs. Omar, I promise we'll take really good care of Marwa and my mom says we can bring her home tomorrow."

Mrs. Omar nodded, and after talking to Marwa some more, and one last look, she went back down the hall to go to work.

Thank goodness Tish had worked everything out with Mrs. Omar the night before. Addie had finally told her everything, mainly because Tish kept pestering her with a million questions. In the end, because Tish had a soft spot for Mr. Norris, she agreed to go along with Addie's plan. She even had an idea about what to do with Mr. Norris's father's papers. She sent an email to Aunt Tina's brother Matt.

"I hope Dickson gets here," said Addie to Marwa. "If he doesn't, then it's only you and Des."

"That's okay," said Marwa. "Des and me, we can do it! You said you have the key for the room in the garage?"

Addie fished in her pocket.

"Here," she said, handing it over. "Mr. Norris told me about the vault before he completely passed out. He said he and his father had cleared out the lab equipment but all his father's files and papers are still there. He said everything has to go. As he tells it, the papers have top secret, classified stuff about the experiments his father worked on. If the information got out, it could be really dangerous. Tell Des to get a hold of Matt. He'll take care of the rest."

Des brought the cart of breakfast trays, and as soon as they were handed out, he and Marwa went off to the garage.

Wilma, who was in on the plan, watched them go.

"You think this plan of yours is going to work?"

"Yes sirree," Addie said, echoing Granny Lu. If there was one thing the Munroes of Mount Repose, Maine, were known for, it was getting things done.

Then, because she wasn't actually sure at all, she went to sit with the residents having breakfast to go over again what she was asking them to do.

It took all morning, explaining again. And again.

Now it was lunchtime. She felt pretty sure most of the residents got it. Mrs. Firillo was a question mark, but Mr. Trippling, who was on his feet again, if a little wobbly, said he'd keep an eye on her. Mrs. Ruckleshaus was ready and willing, thinking it was a game the ship's cruise director had organized. Mrs. Barker was confused about everything, and Mr. Greenberg, well, Addie never knew what he was thinking, but he never spoke anyway.

Fortunately, Mr. Norris had spent the morning in bed. Addie knew that for a fact because she'd been checking on him every fifteen minutes. The HVV doctor had sent in an order for a change to his medications, so hopefully he wouldn't be as groggy. When he was finally up and dressed, he was too scared to come out of his room.

"Come on," said Addie. "I'll stick with you and coach you. You want to be just a normal, nothing-special old guy so that Mrs. Sloat won't think you're crazy. You know, every time you see her you blow up at her, so no wonder she thinks, or hopes, you're losing it. You have to show her you're just an average, friendly, jolly, polite old dude."

"Hold on there," he said, eyeing her. "Did you say 'jolly'?"

"Yes, I did," said Addie, pointing a finger at him. "Look, you don't have to do Santa Claus."

"I'd rather play dead."

"Right, and that would really make Mrs. Sloat's day!"

He sighed and got to his feet. He went to the mirror over his bureau, gave his hair a quick comb, and buttoned his jacket.

"Think about it as if you're putting on a play," said Addie. "Be polite like Mr. Trippling, friendly like Mrs. Firillo, add in some laughing like Mrs. A, C, and D, and be sharp like Minerva."

He groaned.

She took his arm and walked him down the hall.

"You're going to knock Mrs. Sloat for a loop."

"That's the only enjoyment I'll get out of this," he grumbled.

They got to the dining room, which was filling up with residents for lunch.

"Okay, take it away, Mr. Norris." Addie gave him a little push.

For a moment, he looked terrified, as everyone turned to look at him. Then, as Miss Trotter edged past him to her table, he followed and pulled out her chair for her.

Minerva was sitting at the next table and motioned to a chair for him. Mrs. Firillo and Mr. Trippling waved and smiled to him. Addie was watching from the doorway.

After a deep breath, there was a tremor at the corners of Mr. Norris's mouth. His face screwed up in concentration. Muscles stretched and pulled this way, then that way, until his lips widened into something never before seen. He even gave a little wave back.

"Addie, I'm here! I made it!"

Dickson arrived out of breath.

"Addie, I couldn't call you, but my mom was coming this morning anyway for the nursery school visit. And then we're staying for the party. What did you want?"

"Come over here, Dickson. I've got a ton to tell you."

As she launched into what had happened the night before and her plan for Mr. Norris, Dickson's eyes began to bulge so much she remembered she used to call him Bug Boy. He peeked into the dining room.

"Wow, he's...laughing? And chatting?"

"I know, I hope it doesn't kill him," said Addie. "So far, so good, but the real test will be when your mother comes."

As lunch was winding down, people began to leave

the dining room. Mr. Norris walked out listening to Mrs. Firillo telling a story, but when he saw Addie and Dickson he came over to them.

"How long do I need to keep this up?" He glared at Addie through a plastered-on smile.

"Long enough to convince Mrs. Sloat and Marcus Fox and Obsidian."

"Hey, Mr. Norris," Dickson said quietly, studying his feet. "I know I said way too much and gave you away. You'll probably never forgive me, but I'll make sure no one will find anything in your vault, and I mean ANYTHING, that they can use against you."

Mr. Norris scowled at him and didn't say a word.

Wilma was reminding residents the nursery school would be coming by soon for their Halloween visit and the HVV party would be that evening. She came up to Mr. Norris.

"Well, I have to say that was one of the most pleasant lunchtime experiences we've had on Arborvine, Mr. Norris." She lowered her voice. "Mrs. Ruckleshaus wanted to know who the charming new gentleman was and asked to eat with you some night."

Mr. Norris stared at Wilma, then shot his eyes sideways at Addie.

"You're doing a great job, Mr. Norris," whispered Dickson before turning to Addie and giving her a thumbs-up. "Good plan. I'll go find Marwa and Des and Matt and be back as soon as everything's cleaned up. You can count on me, Mr. Norris!" He stood at attention, gave a salute, and took off.

Residents came by to say hello to Mr. Norris, who had sunk into one of the lounge's easy chairs.

"Oh, Mr. Norris," said Mr. Trippling, holding on to Mrs. Firillo. "Patsy and I were just saying we should sign up to go together on the HVV van to the orchestra." He finished with a wink to Mr. Norris.

Mr. Norris managed a nod.

"Oh, that would be fun." He wasn't completely convincing.

Addie nudged him.

"Come on," whispered Addie. "Keep smiling.

"Mrs. Firillo," she said, "could Mr. Norris pat Izzy?"

Mrs. Firillo looked horrified.

"Oh, no, dearie, he doesn't like—"

Mr. Trippling elbowed her.

"Oh, that's right, I forgot. Silly me!" She laughed. "Well, if you think so..."

She held Izzy out toward Mr. Norris.

With a faint growl, Mr. Norris stuck out a hand and tapped Izzy on the head. Twice.

While they all waited around the lounge for the nursery school to come show off their costumes, others came by to see Mr. Norris. There was a lot of winking going on between the Mrs. A, C, and D. They giggled and whispered and told Mr. Norris over and over how well he was looking.

Miss Trotter brought Mr. Greenberg by in his wheelchair. Watching the two men sit and stare at each other was like looking at mirror images. Except Mr. Norris kept his weird, painful smile glued to his face. Mr.

Greenberg gave him a wink and a thumbs-up before Miss Trotter wheeled him away.

She let out a shy little snicker as she passed Addie.

"I think it's rather thrilling being part of this conspiracy."

Wilma clapped her hands.

"The nursery school is here, folks. How about if everyone takes a seat and we'll make room for the kids to parade around."

A mini-mob came down the hallway with a cluster of parents escorted by Mrs. Sloat, Dr. Barker, and Babs Duckworthy, who was snapping pictures of everyone.

Mrs. Sloat was doing her best to beam at everyone while adjusting the silk scarf covering her bandaged head.

A mother led the children single file around the seated adults.

"Grandma!" she said when she got to Genevieve Barker. "Here's little Genevieve...your great-granddaughter!"

"No, I'm not," said the little girl. "I'm a squirrel, Mommy! You said you'd remember!"

Dr. Barker approached.

"And a very fine squirrel you are, Genevieve! Tell your great-grandma what you've got in your paws."

The little squirrel handed Mrs. Barker a card.

"I made a picture of you and a flower and a bee."

Genevieve Barker smiled sweetly and looked at the card.

"Which one is me?"

The rest of the parade consisted of three ninjas, a

witch who was making scary faces at the mermaid, a stegosaurus with a tail so long it tripped the princess and the ghost, and a pumpkin who was in tears because someone said she looked like a butternut squash.

There were also, of course, tiny superheroes.

Spidey was doing his spider poses and Superman was flying up and down the hall as fast as his little feet would go.

"Are they all dwarves?" muttered Mr. Norris.

A ninja had come to a standstill in front of him and was eyeing the bag of candy corn the princess had given Mr. Norris.

Mrs. Sloat edged him aside.

"Mr. Norris." She cleared her throat. "I heard about last night." With a flourish, her hand went to the bandage on her head. "In case you want to know, they had to SHAVE part of my head! But never mind. We will discuss what happened later."

She lost her train of thought as she took in his wide, slightly lopsided smile beaming up at her. She watched, transfixed, as he happily popped candy corn piece by piece into his mouth with a "Yum!"

He held up the bag of candy corn to her.

"Want some?"

Addie, sitting beside him, patted him on the back.

"Mrs. Sloat, Mr. Norris has been feeling really great today."

Mrs. Sloat bent down and peered into his face, the way someone looks in a window to see who's there.

Minerva wheeled up on Ruby.

"Hello, Mrs. Sloat. Mr. Norris, let's finish our conversation later about the stock market. It was so interesting what you were saying about why the Chinese political situation is expected to drive up technology stocks by twenty percent."

Mr. Norris gave his best chuckle and said, "Absolutely. Looking forward to it." He gave a merry little wave as Minerva whirred off to her room. Mrs. Sloat was left staring after her.

Her attention was brought back to Mr. Norris.

"Candy corn at Halloween, Mrs. Sloat," he said sweetly, "brings back such happy memories. Did you know it was first made in the 1880s by a candy company in Philadelphia? And I've read that today, almost thirty-five million pounds of it are sold every year. Think of that."

After a long, squinty-eyed look at him, Mrs. Sloat high-heeled it off to the nurses' station. The nurses had told Addie they couldn't lie but would go along with her plan as much as they could.

While Mrs. Sloat was conferring with them, and the nursery school children were handing out their cards, Marwa and Dickson came in the terrace door.

"We did it!" Marwa whispered with a thumbs-up. "There were so many papers! We filled eight trash bags!"

"Addie," said Dickson with a scowl. "I want you to know what it took for me to get rid of those papers with numbers and graphs and stuff all over them and not keep them to look at!"

"Thanks, Dickson. I bet it was hard. But it'll help keep Mr. Norris safe."

Mr. Norris looked up. For a second, the real Mr. Norris was back in town.

"Are you sure? Everything is gone?"

"Everything," said Marwa. "We did a really good job, Mr. Norris." She looked toward the terrace door. "Do you smell it, Mr. Norris?"

He looked at her, then outside.

"What am I supposed to smell?" he said.

"Well, all I can say," said Marwa with a grin, "is Des and Matt both said it was the perfect day to burn leaves."

Mr. Norris dipped his head and nodded, looking relieved.

The miniature Spidey came by with a cookie.

"Hey, Spider-Man!" called Marwa.

The mini-Spidey struck his spider pose.

"Now THAT'S the way superheroes are supposed to act!"

Mrs. Sloat marched back to Mr. Norris.

"Dr. Mills agrees with me and is ordering a complete evaluation as soon as possible. We will find out everything we need to know." She leaned closer and said in a tight, angry voice, "And we will get to the bottom of what happened yesterday and how I ended up across the room!"

Mr. Norris didn't miss a beat.

"Believe me, Mrs. Sloat, any way I can be of help..." He stood up, straight and tall. "I do apologize. Let me know what I can do."

Mrs. Sloat screwed her eyes up on him.

"Has something changed today, Mr. Norris?"

She put one hand on her hip. Even with her high heels, Mr. Norris towered over her.

"Mr. Norris, I've invited people to the Halloween party later today. Important people. They want to meet with you before the party. Why don't you rest so you'll be feeling your best this afternoon." She glared at Addie.

"Wilma, please have an aide take Mr. Norris back to his room and help him lie down."

"Oh, I'm feeling fine," said Mr. Norris with a grin. "In fact, it's such a nice day I was thinking of fitting in a game of croquet before it gets too cold."

Mrs. Sloat frowned and turned to Dr. Barker.

"Alan, I think it's time for the nursery school to leave. We have to get ready for tonight."

"Wonderful party, everyone!" Dr. Barker clapped his hands and got everyone's attention with his booming voice. "Wonderful party! Wonderful costumes! Thank you all for coming."

Parents picked up broken cookies and squashed cards. They pulled the ninjas and superheroes away, picked up the dinosaur's tail, and calmed the witch.

The last to go was a small group standing around Mrs. A, C, and D.

"We're playing a game!" Mrs. A told the parents. Her eyes sparkled. "They want to know how old we are. What was the last guess?" She looked at Mrs. C and Mrs. D. They laughed.

"Nine thousand!" yelled the princess.

CHAPTER 30

"You were really good, Mr. Norris!" said Marwa a little later.

She bounced onto the foot of his bed. Addie and Dickson were on the floor, where Dickson was untangling a beach-ball-sized mess of wire.

Addie laughed.

"Mr. Norris was smiling so much, I think he was channeling you, Marwa!"

"Anyone would think you were just another average old guy," said Dickson without looking up.

"Now," said Addie, "you just need to convince Marcus Fox and his Obsidian company."

Mr. Norris lay slumped back on his pillows.

"When are they coming?"

Dickson looked up from the wire. "My mother said three o'clock."

"I don't know if they'll believe me," said Mr. Norris, his head limp on the pillow, his eyes closed.

"Of course they will. You had everyone in the lounge believing you, even the ones who were in on the secret!" said Addie.

He shook his head.

"You don't know these people. They've gone by different names over the years. They weren't Obsidian when my father knew them, but if they are who I think they are...I've always been afraid they'd show up one day."

"Addie, take this end and hold it." Dickson handed her a wire. "Well, at least we'll be able to hear what they say."

Mr. Norris looked down at the pile of equipment on the floor.

"You really think a microphone and speaker from the 1940s is going to work?"

"Why not?" said Dickson. "You always say they don't make things like they used to!"

Mr. Norris grunted.

Dickson held up an old-fashioned steel microphone, which looked like a mini junkyard version of R2-D2.

"The minute I saw this in the garage, I knew it would be useful sooner or later! Isn't it so cool? But we'll need to hide it somewhere."

"I know!" said Marwa. "I'll get some of Mrs. Firillo's plants. The microphone can go on the windowsill and we can put the plants around it."

While Marwa worked on hiding the microphone, Dickson ran the wire out the window and into Mrs. D's room next door.

Half an hour later, Dickson had everything set up and ready for a test run. Marwa was in Mrs. D's room huddled with Mrs. A, C, and D around the oversized metallic speaker.

"It's like the good old days," said Mrs. A, "when we used to gather round to listen to radio shows!"

Addie had been keeping Mr. Norris company. He couldn't stay still. He cleared his throat, checked to see if his canes were within reach, took sips of water.

"Addie," he said softly, "you think it will be easy getting rid of these people, but it won't. I know more than you do about what they want."

"You'll be fine," she said. "Be the friendly old guy who doesn't know anything. What can they do about it? And remember, the vault is completely cleared out." She even patted his old hand for emphasis.

Dickson flew in from Mrs. D's room.

"Addie, we've got to go! No time for a test run. Wilma said my mom called to say they were on their way. Mr. Norris, remember to say you can't hear them so they'll speak extra loud."

Dickson gave him a big thumbs-up and dragged Addie out of the room.

She left him with a fierce whisper.

"You can do this!"

She almost ran right into Marcus Fox.

"Addie! Dickson! Hi there!"

Marcus Fox radiated charm.

"Mr. Norris is a little tired," said Addie. "There was the nursery school visit, and then he played croquet."

She didn't have to fake the worried look on her face. Suddenly, she didn't know what to do with her hands or where to look. She could feel Marcus Fox's eyes pinned on her. "Maybe you shouldn't stay very long." Her voice wavered. She couldn't have convinced a fly.

Marcus Fox nodded and beamed.

"Thanks. Good to know."

Then he, along with five women and men, slid into Mr. Norris's room without knocking. Every one of them wore a dark gray business suit. Only Mrs. Sloat wore anything different. She fidgeted in her daffodil-yellow dress as if she guessed she'd made some fatal fashion mistake.

"Dickson dear, I'll see you later at the party," she said, before disappearing into Mr. Norris's room and firmly closing the door.

Addie followed Dickson into Mrs. D's room. Once inside, with the door shut, she couldn't believe what she saw. Not only were Mrs. A, C, and D crouched around the speaker with Marwa, but there were Mr. Trippling, Mrs. Firillo (without Izzy), Wilma, Miss Trotter and Mr. Greenberg in his wheelchair, Mrs. Ruckleshaus, Minerva, Tish, Brad, and Des. And what was more, they were being so quiet, Addie could have heard a tissue drop out of Miss Trotter's sleeve.

Dickson turned the speaker on. A small white light flickered, faded out, flickered again, then pulled itself together into a steady glow.

Scratchy sounds at first, but then voices. Definitely voices. Dickson turned up the volume as much as he dared while every head craned toward the speaker as if it was magnetized.

The deep voice of a man, used to being in charge:

"...It's been a long time, Mr. Norris, but we're here to work with you...."

Loud throat-clearing. Mr. Norris.

"No pictures!" he said.

The man:

"Of course. No pictures. Put your phones away. We just want to have a conversation, ask a few simple questions."

"I can't hear you," Mr. Norris said.

In the next room, Dickson gave Addie and Marwa a thumbs-up and a smile.

"I apologize," said the man. "I'll speak up. Is that better?"

Mr. Norris gave a grunt.

"Why is she looking at me, may I ask, and taking notes?"

A woman:

"I'm a doctor, a specialist in cognitive function, Mr. Norris. We've heard conflicting reports about you, that you haven't been yourself lately but also that you've been absolutely fine. I'd like to assess what exactly is going on."

Marcus Fox broke in.

"All we want is the truth, Mr. Norris. We know... and you know...who you are. We'd like you to come work with us the way your father did."

"My father never worked with you!" Mr. Norris

shouted, before a strangled fit of coughing. "Leave me alone."

The woman:

"We won't keep you long, we're only asking for your cooperation. If you insist on refusing, we will have to look at—"

The man:

"Mrs. Sloat, I'm afraid our organization has certain privacy restrictions. Could we ask you to step outside the room briefly? Thank you. We really appreciate it."

Addie looked around Mrs. D's room, held her finger up to her lips, and pointed to the hallway...where Mrs. Sloat would probably be waiting.

Dickson lowered the volume a notch.

The voices next door started up again. The man took the lead.

"Mr. Norris, the work your father did—"

"And my grandfather," Marcus Fox cut in. "Who never got the credit he deserved."

"Yes, of course, the work THEY did was the most advanced, revolutionary work seen in generations. It was so far outside the realm of legitimate science that no one understood it...at that time. But we always believed, and, with your help, we want to pursue what they started." He lowered his voice. "And you, Mr. Norris, you were a witness to some of it...weren't you?"

Silence.

"Of course, your father rather unfortunately left the organization over a misunderstanding, and then there was the tragic accident. We tried to help, but your father refused. And then...I don't know what he was thinking...he destroyed everything. He did, didn't he? The lab?"

Mr. Norris was heard to mumble:

"Don't know what you're talking about."

"Maybe we can help you to remember—" came the woman's silky voice.

Marcus Fox interrupted.

"Don't forget, the research was funded by the original organization. They have a claim to any discoveries."

"I can't help you. It was a long time ago."

"I know," soothed the woman, "only a few more minutes."

"Actually," said the man, "I don't think we should bother Mr. Norris any more today. If we could just take a look at whatever papers you have of your father's, that would be enough for now and we'd leave you alone. How does that sound?"

"Mr. Norris?" said the woman. "The papers?"

"Come on." Marcus Fox sounded angry. "Just tell us where they are. After all, it was my grandfather's research too!"

"Let's take it easy," said the man. There was whispering.

Addie heard something like "Try those drawers over there...."

"You know," the man went on, while the listeners heard faint sounds of drawers and closets being opened and closed, "it's taken a long time to find you. We traced the leads we had on Breathalyzer to several continents.

We heard you'd changed your name, or you'd died. It wasn't until we pried a bit of information from a former associate of the Guild..."

Next door, Dickson whipped around to look at the others. He mouthed, "The Guild?" wide-eyed at Marwa.

"...but they said you were no longer a member."

There was a rasp of a laugh from Mr. Norris and a sudden flurry of whispers.

Two of the people must have been standing near the microphone, because their whispers came in loud and clear.

"Keys..."

"Mr. Norris?" said the man briskly. "We're going to leave you alone and let you rest. Think about what I've said. We'll be back in a little while."

A door was heard to open, and voices faded down the hall. The listeners waited in Mrs. D's room for four long minutes. When no one could stand it any longer, Mrs. D was sent to peek out her door.

"All clear!" she said.

Dickson tumbled into Mr. Norris's room and exploded. "YOU BELONGED TO THE GUILD?!"

Mr. Norris lay on his rumpled bed exactly how they had left him. He looked gray and empty. The shell of an old man.

"What's the Guild?" Addie asked Marwa.

Marwa turned to her, awestruck.

"Only the most amazing league of superheroes there is!"

A grumble came from the bed.

"They're not *that* amazing."

"Excuse me?" Dickson's voice was close to shrieking. "You can't get any more amazing than the Guild! Come on, Mr. Norris, we're talking about THE GUILD here!"

Mr. Norris turned on his side, facing the wall.

"You only know the crap you've heard," he growled. "You don't know about their silly rules, what you have to do to be a member, the dress code and the meetings that go on for days!" He swore under his breath. "The sub-committees, the paperwork, you kids have no idea how easy you have it!"

Addie had to sit down. She slumped on the floor, leaning back against the wall. Having something solid behind her felt good. All this talk about superheroes was making her dizzy. It was one thing for kids, but for grown-ups to calmly discuss superheroes as if they really existed? This couldn't be real, it couldn't be happening. The world was going crazy. Nothing should be more real and boring than an old dude's room in an old folks' home, but when she tuned in to the conversation again, Dickson, Marwa, and Mr. Norris were still deep in a discussion about the Guild.

Addie had had enough.

"You guys, cut it out! Are you all crazy? Superheroes, the Guild, come on...IT'S...NOT...REAL! Nothing is going to change the way things ARE, don't you get it?"

Dickson and Marwa looked at her in shock.

There was silence. Until Mr. Norris heaved himself up from his bed.

"Addie's right. Nothing is going to change if we just sit here and talk about it." He breathed in and rubbed his eyes. "It's the last thing I want to do, but it's time to contact the Guild. Hand me the phone, Dickson," he said, standing up.

Dickson stared at him, speechless.

"THE PHONE?" whispered Marwa. "You can call the Guild on...THE PHONE?"

Mr. Norris fumbled with the cordless phone.

"If I can remember the number...It's been so long, maybe they've changed it. The idiots. It would be just like them." He punched in numbers. "Dickson, keep an eye on the hallway. When they find the vault's empty, they'll be back."

Listening to the phone, Mr. Norris rolled his eyes.

"Of course, a recording, wouldn't you know it! Everyone's so busy saving the world, there's no one to pick up the phone?"

Dickson charged over to Mr. Norris.

"A recording...from the Guild? Who is it? What do they say? I want to hear it!"

Dickson pulled on Mr. Norris's jacket to make him bend down. He and Marwa inched their ears as close to the phone as they could get. Addie didn't have the strength or the desire to move. She stayed where she was on the floor, her head tilted back, her eyes closed.

Mr. Norris was finishing the message he was leaving when a voice from the doorway interrupted him.

"Well, Mr. Norris, we're back sooner than we thought. Let's hang up the phone, shall we?"

A man with sparse gray hair and thin lips stood in the doorway watching Mr. Norris. The man's voice was cold and commanding, the same voice they'd heard from the speaker. It made Addie shiver.

Slowly, Mr. Norris straightened up to his full height. He seemed to tower over the man in the doorway.

"You didn't find anything of interest?"

A glimmer of a smile cut across the thin lips of the man. Marcus Fox and the five men and women had gathered behind him. Though he was smaller than Mr. Norris, the man had the pale eyes and unblinking stare of a cat who could pounce at any second.

"Oh, it was interesting to see the vault in the garage... even though it's empty. You'll tell us where the papers are in time. But in the end, they're not that important to us." He and Mr. Norris looked long and hard at each other. The energy in the room could almost be heard snapping and crackling. And then, so softly Addie had to strain to hear, the man said, "You can guess what we want."

Addie held her breath. Everyone turned to stone as they waited to see what Mr. Norris or the older man would do next.

Until, pushing her way through the dark gray cluster, in sprang Mrs. Sloat. Mrs. Sloat, in daffodil yellow, ready to dazzle her newfound investors from Obsidian, who, she was sure, would put Happy Valley Village on the map once and for all.

"Come, everyone, it's time for the party!"

CHAPTER 31

The Halloween party was a big deal for Mrs. Sloat, so she had ordered everyone to attend. Most of the residents of Arborvine were already at the party. The last stragglers on the hall were being rounded up and herded toward the main building as Dickson and Marwa snuck off to change into their costumes.

Mrs. Sloat insisted on leading Mr. Norris and the Obsidian group herself.

"Wait till you see the decorations!" She was giving her best beaming sales pitch to the Obsidian crowd. "This will give you a chance to see Happy Valley Village at its finest! And this year, our theme is...SUPERHEROES! But not your well-known superheroes, because, to tell the truth"—she lowered her voice—"not all our residents know a lot about superheroes. No, this is a 'Be Your Own Superhero' party...you know, to build self-esteem and all that business."

The Obsidian group couldn't have cared less. As they moved down the hallway, weaving around scooters and walkers, they jostled to surround Mr. Norris and Addie. It seemed like they were trying to separate the two of them, but Addie held tight to Mr. Norris.

Mr. Norris looked nervous.

"Slow down," she said to the Obsidian people pushing from behind. "Mr. Norris can't walk that fast."

One of them chuckled.

"Oh, really? You want us to believe that?"

There was a squash of people at the elevators. Even using two of them plus the service elevator, it would take some time.

Mr. Norris looked unusually hot and was breathing fast.

"I hate crowds like this," he muttered.

"Breathe...slowly," Addie whispered.

To entertain her guests, Mrs. Sloat kept up the commentary.

"We asked everyone to dress accordingly and come up with some 'superpower' they have. So, Wilma, what is your superpower?"

Wilma finished tying a resident's shoe and straightened up. She'd painted a large red T-shirt with WONDER WOMAN WILMA.

"Well, I can coax a pill down the throat of an eighty-nine-year-old woman who swears she can't swallow pills, talk an exercise-hater into trying a yoga class, and still be their friend at the end of the day. How's that?"

Mrs. Sloat frowned momentarily, then brightened.

"Wonderful!" She laughed. "Wonder Woman Wilma! Oh, here's the elevator."

As hard as Addie tried to avoid it, she found herself in an elevator with only Mr. Norris and the Obsidian people. They'd maneuvered their way in at the last minute, edging past a woman with a walker who was taking her time.

The doors closed. Addie and Mr. Norris were wedged in on all sides. He looked like he was going to faint.

"Mr. Norris," said the man in charge, "you know how important this is. Important to science, important to your father's work. We need to see what abilities you received from the radiation exposure, before it's too late."

"You mean before I die," growled Mr. Norris, wiping his forehead.

The man tightened his thin lips and ignored the comment.

"Your father died from the accident. You didn't. You survived, but with special powers. Think what a discovery like this would mean for the human race! If we could determine how you gained your superpowers, and then find a way to duplicate it..."

"And think what a catastrophe it would be if we couldn't study you," said a woman. "You must understand..." Her voice was smooth and silky, but her face was hard as granite. Addie guessed she was the one who'd said she was a doctor.

"I don't believe for one second you're thinking about the human race!" Mr. Norris was panting. "How stupid do you think I am? You're only thinking about yourselves. You want to experiment and run tests on me like a lab specimen!"

"We would, of course, compensate you, or consider any number of ways to make it worth your while, if you'll only come with us—"

The elevator doors opened on Mrs. Sloat, who, distressed at having lost her star guests, brightened up instantly when she saw them.

"There you are!"

Mr. Norris and Addie tumbled out of the elevator with the rest of them and were swept along as Mrs. Sloat led the parade down the main hall, past the auditorium and main dining room. Tables lining the hallway were crowded with trays of shrimp, chicken wings, vegetables with dips, beef on sticks, sausage in mushroom caps, and baby pizzas. The dessert tables were loaded with carrot cakes, mini-cheesecakes, bite-sized pumpkin and pecan pies. And wedged into the few empty spots left were baskets of Halloween candy.

"Please, help yourselves," said Mrs. Sloat. "Des, can I have some plates for our guests?"

Des wore his kitchen uniform with an old leather racing car driver's helmet and goggles.

He handed paper plates to Mrs. Sloat. It was kind of hard to see him through the goggles, but Addie thought she saw him wink.

While Mrs. Sloat heaped food on the Obsidian group's plates even as most were trying to refuse, Mr. Norris looked ahead to the crowded atrium and groaned.

"Any ideas for how to get out of this mess?" he whispered to Addie. "I'm going to pass out if I have to go in there. And please, don't tell me I have to put on some stupid costume!"

"We don't have time for costumes," said Addie. "I mean, a costume is what you wear when you pretend to be someone else. I wanted you to pretend to be just a nice old guy, but you had a hard time doing that in the elevator just now!"

"How could I not argue with them? You heard what they said! It was a good idea, but I think they've figured it out. We need plan B."

"Plan B is to keep you away from them…and you'll be safer in a crowd." She looked at him, thinking. "If they wanted you badly enough…would they just kidnap you?"

"What do you think?"

"Yeah, that's what I thought. Okay," she said, "plan B."

She grabbed hold of his sleeve and pulled him into the crush of people. Two of the strongest-looking men from Obsidian followed close behind but didn't stop them.

They entered the atrium that had been transformed with all the decorations. The ceiling soared overhead to the skylights, which were dark in the October evening. The only light came from the tiny orange and white lights hanging from the ceiling and walls and the flickering lights inside carved pumpkin faces. A lone spotlight lit up a fiddle player, one foot up on a hay bale, playing in a corner.

"We found you!" Two voices screamed in Addie's ear.

One was Marwa, wearing most of what she had in her closet. Addie knew she was "Ms. Marwa!" ("No relation to Ms. Marvel.") The other was Dickson, who was a...

"You don't know?" he shrieked. Addie shook her head. He was wearing what looked like an old gray laundry bag with holes cut in it.

"A slug! Isn't it obvious? I'll slime you to death!" He held up a container. "It's glow-in-the-dark glitter slime!"

Mr. Norris cleared his throat.

"Could we...?"

Addie filled Marwa and Dickson in on Obsidian and pointed out the two guys keeping an eye on them. One was talking on his cell phone.

"This could be bad," said Dickson, bug-eyed.

"Really bad," said Marwa.

"We need to keep Obsidian away from Mr. Norris, so..." Addie looked around the darkened room with everyone in their crazy costumes. "Pass the word along: Obsidian can't take Mr. Norris. They're easy to spot because they're all in the same dark clothes. That'll give us time until—"

"The Guild shows up!" cried Dickson.

Addie looked at him.

"Dickson, they're not showing up!" she hissed, low enough so that Mr. Norris couldn't hear. "It was just some random number Mr. Norris called and left a message! Don't be such a dreamer! It's up to us. Now, go tell people."

Dickson and Marwa flew off like the junior superheroes they were.

"In the meantime, while you're collecting your troops," said Mr. Norris slowly, "you might take a look at the door."

Addie couldn't see as well as he could over the tops of heads, but she got a glimpse between a ghost and a caped crusader. Men and women, maybe ten of them, in the same dark gray tracksuit, were filing in. Wearing headsets, they lined up inside, blocking the door, and surveyed the crowd.

Addie's heart sank. There were enough people from Obsidian now to do whatever they wanted. Even if they were far outnumbered by the partygoers, each one looked like they could mow down thirty residents apiece.

Suddenly, a red scooter whirred to a stop right in front of the Obsidian wall. Addie couldn't miss the shining aluminum-foil helmet. And she couldn't stop the smile spreading across her face. She grabbed Mr. Norris.

"Minerva! She was coming as the Greek goddess Minerva. Miss Trotter helped her make that helmet, and her spear is an old broom handle."

Right behind her came Wonder Woman Wilma, striding like a force of nature. Then Miss Trotter, dressed in a long, pleated white sheet covered in glitter, pushed Mr. Greenberg in his wheelchair. He was very convincing in his cardboard-cutout costume as the Sphinx because he never moved. Miss Trotter parked the wheelchair next to the scooter, hemming in more of the dark gray line. She wore a magnificent wig she must have made and exotic eye makeup.

"Wow, she's Cleopatra!" said Addie. "I can't believe it!" She'd never seen Miss Trotter look happier.

Mrs. Ruckleshaus elbowed her way through. She was dressed as a mermaid with a tail made out of bubble wrap, and from a container, she blew bubbles in the Obsidian faces.

Most of the residents didn't realize what was happening and continued to enjoy the party, but Addie could see a small but growing number assembling in front of the Obsidian people.

"Hey, sweetie, where do you want me?" Tish (also known as Ultraviolet) appeared beside them with purple hair and a skintight leotard covered in tattoo images. "Mr. Norris, are you feeling okay? You look a little..."

"I'm feeling better watching those stinkers squirm."

"Maybe you could go keep an eye on Mrs. A, C, and D," said Addie.

"Mmm, looks like they're getting a little giddy. Did you hear what their costumes are? Instead of superHEROES...they're a superMARKET! That's why the shopping baskets and plastic fruit. They've been laughing about it for days. Okay, I'm off." But then Tish turned back. "Hey, you two, be careful. You need anything, just holler. We'll make these creeps go away. Don't worry." And she disappeared into the crowd.

Babs Duckworthy rushed by with two local reporters.

"Mr. Norris, we'll catch up with you shortly, but we have to interview those strange people at the door first. I don't know who they are or what they think they're doing here!"

She wore an old-fashioned suit and clunky glasses with a pencil stuck behind one ear. The notebook she carried said LOIS LANE, GIRL REPORTER.

Dr. Barker, in his naval uniform, pushed Mrs. Barker along in her wheelchair in Babs's wake to personally inspect the commotion at the door.

The crowd at the door grew louder and more chaotic. The residents were causing a regular ruckus. The two Obsidian guys who had been trailing Addie and Mr. Norris went to help.

As Addie watched them go, she noticed a bunch of kids at Mr. Norris's elbow, their eyes glued to him in wonder and awe.

"Marshall?"

He was dressed as a basketball player with the same vomit-yellow shorts he paraded at school. By his side were other boys and girls, among them the famous Lucas, who Dickson had punched.

"What are you guys doing here?" Addie couldn't believe it. Of all the times for these bozos to show up!

Marshall didn't move.

"Is that HIM?" he whispered.

Mr. Norris shifted his weight and tapped one cane on the floor like he was about to bolt.

"Come on, Addie, is this the guy?"

Dickson arrived, breathless.

"Whoa, what are you guys doing here? Never mind. I've got to find Brad. Addie, have you seen him? Those people refuse to move, even for Dr. Barker! We need Brad. He could kick some crap out of them. Where is he?" Dickson said, looking around. "He's calling himself the Flash-Light and wearing tons of...I don't see him. Have you seen him?"

Marshall stepped up.

"You need some muscle, dude? For those guys by the door? Yeah, Lucas and me saw them. They're serious stuff. But we can handle them, right, Lucas?"

"Sure!" said Lucas, whipping out his plastic double-blade ninja sword and silver rubber throwing stars. "Anything for Truth and Justice!"

With one last starstruck gaze at Mr. Norris, they took off, shouting, "Pow!" "Crack!" "Thwap!" "Crunch!" "Oof!" and "Gaagh!"

Addie gave Mr. Norris's sleeve a tug.

"With what's going on at the door, let's you and me disappear. Okay?"

They were backing away, easing quietly past the fiddle player, when angry barks let loose behind them.

"Izzy, dearie, hush!" Mrs. Firillo picked up her little bundle of joy and held her tight, but the terrier was going berserk. She squirmed and barked at everything in sight. Gene Trippling did what he could, but nothing could stop Izzy. "It's only Mr. Norris and Addie. They didn't mean to scare you."

Mr. Trippling rolled his eyes to the ceiling.

"I told you not to bring her to the party!"

"But we needed her for our costume."

"Well, I think it's our costumes that are freaking her out!"

He and Mrs. Firillo were covered in plastic vines.

Mr. Trippling looked at Mr. Norris and Addie.

"She talked me into being a superhero named Venus Flytrap!" He grumbled. "Guess what the dog is." Izzy wore a pair of limp wings. "Wish it was for real," he grumbled.

"Oh, Gene, stop! Now look what you've done. She's beside herself. It's all these people. Izzy, stop squirming!"

But Izzy had had enough of the party and her costume. She wriggled and barked and squirmed until Mrs. Firillo set her on the floor. And the minute those little paws touched down, Izzy took off, her leash disappearing behind her like a snake.

"Izzy!" screamed Mrs. Firillo.

"I can get her," said Addie. She crouched down and beetled her way through the crowd. She was making good progress and knew she was getting close. The barks were just ahead, somewhere through the legs and capes and boots.

There it was! The end of the leash on the floor. She made a grab for it and followed it up...to where Izzy was pinned in the arms of Marcus Fox. He had his hand expertly clamped around Izzy's muzzle so she couldn't bark. Izzy was seething. He was smiling.

Strong hands from behind gripped Addie's shoulders and arms.

CHAPTER 32

Addie tried to wriggle free, but two men held her tight, while the man with the pinched lips and the woman with the silky voice stood in front of her. Addie wasn't going anywhere.

"Let's go see Mr. Norris, shall we?" said the man in her ear. "Nice and easy, or the dog will get hurt."

He and the woman pushed Addie along through the crowd, most of whom were unaware of what was going on. She could hear the man talking on his phone. Within seconds there were more dark-suited people around them, all moving together across the room.

"Izzy, my darling! You bad, bad girl!" cried Mrs. Firillo, reaching for the dog. Then she caught sight of who was holding her. "Give her to me at once. I don't want to have anything to do with you. I know you're not my great-nephew. You're...you're...the very worst kind of person!"

Once she was holding Izzy, she turned her back on Marcus Fox the way an opera singer on a grand stage would have done and started off, clutching Izzy to her chest. Mr. Trippling, before he was dragged along in the tangle of vines, gave Marcus Fox a poisonous look.

"You will never, ever, contact Patsy Firillo again!"

Then it was just them, an island of Mr. Norris and Addie, Marcus Fox, the thin-lipped man, and the woman inside a ring of dark gray as the swirl of the Halloween party went on around them.

"Here's what we're going to do...until you decide to cooperate," said Marcus Fox to Mr. Norris. "We're taking Addie." Two Obsidian men held her by her arms. As hard as she tried, she couldn't get free. "It's your choice. Let us know when you're ready to talk."

"We could always try to duplicate your father's experiment on her," said the woman, as if she'd just thought of it, "and see what happens."

"You wouldn't do that!" said Mr. Norris with a gasp. "You...you don't know what would happen!" In the dim light, he looked wild and frightened like one of the flickering pumpkin faces nearby.

"No, you're right, we don't," the woman went on. "That's why we need you to work with us."

"I am never going to work with you!" Mr. Norris was having trouble catching his breath. "I will never help you! And you will not take Addie!"

"But there's the problem," said the pinched-lipped man viciously. "You can't stop us."

He signaled to the team surrounding them. They

closed in on Addie. She was barely visible inside the dark gray ring. They began moving her toward the door.

"You don't know!" Mr. Norris yelled after them. It seemed to take every last bit of his energy. "If you don't let her go, you don't know what you're asking for!"

They didn't stop or even turn to look at him.

Then he started breathing. Not normal, everyday breathing, but breathing in a way that moved air in and out like gusts of wind. It was soft and slow at first. A breeze. But it picked up fast, like a thunderstorm sweeping in over hills and fields.

The ring of gray around Addie turned as the sound grew louder. The Obsidian people parted enough that she was able to see him.

Mr. Norris stood alone in the atrium. Anyone near him had backed away at the strange sounds coming from him. The chatter and fiddle music stopped.

"Don't do it!" Addie cried. "Don't even pretend to do it, or they'll think you really do have superpowers."

He looked at her. The wind died down. It was close to silent among the crowd. Shadows and lights flickered across faces.

"If you make it look like you have superpowers, they might think you really do!" she called to him across the room.

He smiled at her.

"I know them, Addie. I know what they'll do. There's no other way. I have to try."

"No, don't!"

But he had closed his eyes and started breathing

again. Steadying himself, he put all his energy into it. Each breath got stronger and lasted longer. At first, a paper napkin floated up like a leaf; then hair blew across people's faces in ribbons. Soon, there were paper plates and flowers swirling by. Strings of lights flew like whips.

The wind blew harder. People struggled to hold on to their costumes. Capes flew off. People had trouble staying on their feet. They held on to each other as they were swept back against the walls.

Mr. Norris turned in a circle so that the wind blew everyone away from him in all directions. He stood alone in the center. Everyone else spun and tripped and flailed backward. Addie hit the wall next to a zombie and a mummy whose wrappings were blowing like streamers.

The wind took on a roar like a hurricane. It was all around, making it hard to think of anything else. In fact, it was hard to think of anything at all. Shielding her face against the plastic cups, flowers and pieces of food, she had a dim memory of Mr. Norris standing on the tower saying something about working on a superpower that made people forget. A superpower... The memory was fading fast, but in the last second, before it was completely fuzzy and gone, she knew it was him! Mr. Norris was doing it! He was really and truly...

And then there was nothing.

She came to in the dark. Or almost dark. The tiny orange and white lights had mostly hung on to the walls. They were still. The wind had died down. She looked at the collapsed zombie next to her and the shambles of the mummy on the other side. Everyone was slowly waking up and getting to their feet.

She remembered Mr. Norris and looked where she'd seen him last. In fact, she was remembering everything. She remembered the fuzzy feeling of memories slipping away, of nothing left, but now they all came back.

What had happened? Where was he?

She went toward the center of the atrium. It was so hard to see, she almost tripped over him. Mr. Norris lay at her feet in a heap.

Her insides clutched. No...

But then there was a twitch. And she saw one very black, very intense eye fixed on her.

"Didn't I...tell you...I was no good at this?"

She knelt down.

"Are you okay?"

He gave a slight nod.

"Tired out...can't do it."

"But you almost did! You did do it...for a little bit!" She smiled and shook her head. "I don't believe it. You really are..."

CHAPTER 33

Sometimes it only takes an instant for everything to change.

Hands like iron pincers hauled Addie to her feet.

"Nice try, Norris," said Marcus Fox. "Very impressive."

The thin-lipped man focused his pale eyes on Mr. Norris and cleared his throat.

"You are...truly...a superhero. I...can't begin to say how awed I am and—"

"We're taking you with us," cut in the woman. "You"—she signaled to several dark gray suits—"pick him up. Now! Before these oldsters know what's going on. Leave the girl. Put him in the van."

"No, you can't just take him like that!" cried Addie.

Dickson was suddenly by her side.

"Mr. Norris, use your powers again! Don't let them do it!"

Mr. Norris looked at Dickson as two guys dragged him to his feet.

"Wish I could, Dickson, just for you...but I'm all done in."

Addie, Dickson, and Marwa did everything they could, but the gray suits were unbeatable. They pulled Mr. Norris steadily along, even though they were attacked by a ferocious band of fourth and fifth graders, the goddess Minerva, a mermaid, Cleopatra and the Sphinx, and Wonder Woman Wilma.

Obsidian was wading through them all with Mr. Norris in the middle when suddenly the air split open with a ZZZ—AAPP! and something like a fireball flamed over the tops of their heads, hit the far wall in a shower of sparks, and lit a hay bale on fire. A second later, another fireball shot past, sizzling and crackling. It sliced one of the buffet tables in two.

There were shrieks and screams. In the smoke and flames, everyone panicked.

Dickson, in a voice Addie had never heard before, whispered, "Who's that...up there?'

Addie and Marwa looked up. At first Addie thought it was just another shadow.

"OMG," breathed Marwa. "Who else crawls up walls?"

There was a rush of air beside them. Addie turned. She was eye to eye with the shiniest pair of red boots she had ever seen. A figure had leapt onto the reception desk. He towered above them, his hands on his hips, his red cape billowing around him.

"Hey, kids, can you point me to Breathalyzer?"

Dickson tried to talk but could only make gulping noises.

Marwa bounced up and down like a Ping-Pong ball.

"Over there! He's over there!"

She screamed and pointed and bounced.

The man floated down, light as a feather, walked over as people parted before him, and took Mr. Norris out of Obsidian's hands. They started to resist, but he made some kind of ray come out of his eyes and they crumpled around him like bowling pins.

Dickson was swaying, as if he could barely stay on his feet.

"Muscular manipulation!"

Another fireball zinged past, blew the front doors open, and hit one of Obsidian's SUVs. Addie, Marwa, and Dickson turned to see where it had come from. A woman wearing a suit the colors of flames stood beside them.

Dickson sighed as if he was having the best dream ever.

"Energy blast," he murmured.

"I would say we have about two seconds before the sprinkler system kicks in, kids," said the woman. "I'm going to herd the bad guys into their cars. How about if you tell everyone to go back to their rooms—otherwise they're gonna get soaked." She gave them each a thumbs-up.

A man in a black cape and black mask appeared out of the shadows beside her. Marwa, still bouncing, pummeled Dickson on the shoulder. There was a yellow-and-black emblem on the man's chest.

"Nice work, kids. I mean it," he said. "Oh, one more thing, would you tell Breathalyzer to get a cell phone? We couldn't call him back and he didn't leave his number!" He shook his head. "These old guys…"

Sure enough, the sprinklers kicked on. Water sprayed everywhere. Addie, Dickson, and Marwa helped the HVV staff hurry people back to their apartments and rooms. Mrs. Ruckleshaus, wearing her life preserver, told everyone to "Keep calm and carry on"…to the lifeboat stations.

"We're helping the superheroes! No one will believe it when I tell them!" said Marwa.

Addie went to Mr. Norris. Wilma was shoveling him into a wheelchair.

"Let's get you home," said Wilma. "Wonder Woman Wilma is going to make sure you get a nice hot shower and get to bed. How about some tea, or hot chocolate or some of those crazy stewed prunes you like? Anything you want tonight, Mr. Norris, you can have!"

She patted his back and started to wheel him away.

Addie walked alongside for a bit.

"I don't know what to say," she said.

Mr. Norris reached for her hand.

"There's plenty of time," he said. "We'll talk. Tomorrow. Wilma, wait! Back up! You just passed the dessert table!"

Addie left him in Wilma's care to go back to the atrium. She wanted to find Tish.

Babs Duckworthy limped past with her soggy notebook.

"I don't know what that was all about. The two reporters think we've all gone bonkers! I think maybe we have. Either that, or the punch was lethal."

"Oh my, that was fun!" Miss Trotter, her black eyeliner dripping, wheeled Mr. Greenberg back toward Arborvine. "How about you, Malcolm?" He gave it an unprecedented two thumbs-up.

Behind them came Minerva on Ruby. Her helmet was a little lopsided, but she still carried her spear.

"Well, Adelaide, that was exciting! Tomorrow, will you explain what just happened? For now, I'm going home and pulling the covers over my head. Though," she added with a sly smile, "your red-caped friend said I made an excellent Minerva."

At the front entrance, the Obsidian people were bundled into their SUVs (one was still smoldering) and took off with a superhero escort. The red-caped gentleman and the woman wearing flames were flying, the wall-crawler stuck to the lead car's roof, and at the rear roared a shiny black race car. Before the superhero wearing flames left for good, she turned and shot one last fireball at the front entrance.

Mrs. Sloat, who had scraped herself off the floor and dripped her way to the door to say some kind of farewell to her guests, shrieked as the fireball hit one of the entrance pillars.

She was yelling at the superheroes to stop ruining her facility and never come back when Dickson shook her arm.

"Mom...Mom, you don't understand! Look!"

He pointed to where the fireball had hit the pillar.

There was a blazing shield, still smoking, imprinted on the pillar. Underneath the Guild's insignia, it read, THESE PREMISES ARE UNDER THE PROTECTION AND JURISDICTION OF THE GUILD IN PERPETUITY. VIOLATORS WILL BE PROSECUTED!

"What does that mean?" she said weakly.

"It means HVV is protected by the Guild now...the Guild of Superheroes."

She looked at him, her eyes screwed up, trying to make sense of what he'd said.

"Does Mr. Norris have something to do with this?"

Dickson nodded.

"So, you mean, I can't...?"

"I think, unless you want to get in trouble with the superheroes, you need to leave him alone."

She bit her lip and frowned.

"Sorry, Mom, but I think Obsidian is gone for good."

She gazed at the shield on the pillar and didn't appear to be listening to him. "I'm thinking this would look great on a brochure, and those guys...man, were they good-looking! It wouldn't hurt, would it, to ask them if they'd be willing to pose? Maybe you could ask them?"

Dickson rolled his eyes at Addie as he led his mother away.

"Mom, I'm going to need to teach you about super-heroes."

Marwa came over to Addie and said, "Are you okay?"

Addie nodded, smiling.

They stared at each other for a minute, then they

burst out laughing as they wrapped their arms around each other.

Tish appeared and slid a tattooed arm around each of them.

"Wow! What a crazy night! But mostly, I'm glad you're both okay, along with Mr. Norris and everyone else. I thought it was touch and go there for a minute." She gave Addie and Marwa each a big squeeze. "Wouldn't Granny Lu have loved it?"

CHAPTER
34

Two weeks later, on a Saturday afternoon, Addie and Tish were walking over to Arborvine. Tish had questions for Wilma about the certified nursing assistant program she was interested in. Addie was meeting up with Dickson and Marwa. Mr. Norris had mostly recovered from the night of the Halloween party and said he had a surprise for them.

"Let's go through the main entrance," said Addie, "to see what they're doing."

The entrance and the atrium looked like a construction site, with yellow caution tape everywhere, signs that read HARD HATS REQUIRED and ALL GUESTS USE DOOR TO RIGHT, and piles of debris and tools. In the dusty air, the only thing that shone bright and new was the Guild's shield on the entrance pillar.

Addie could never walk past it without stopping.

"I still can't believe it sometimes," she said with

Tish's arm around her shoulders. "I mean, who would have believed it was true?"

"I know," said Tish. "And here we were taking care of him all this time. Crazy!"

They walked through the empty atrium. Mrs. Sloat was taking full advantage of the reconstruction to redo the atrium and enlarge her office.

"Her office is all torn up," said Addie. "Where did you meet with her the other day?"

Tish laughed.

"A little broom closet of an office. She hates it! But it helped keep the meeting short. I came in, she handed me my job review, said I could stay on, and I left. Short and sweet." Tish smiled and shook her head. "She said she wants to forget that the past month's 'complications' ever happened."

Arborvine had finished with Halloween and was now on to Thanksgiving. Mr. Greenberg had a hand-painted paper turkey taped to his door. Next to it were taped pencil sketches. Addie took a closer look. They were of a tall man, hands on his hips, standing in his red boots with a cape flowing around him, someone crawling on the wall like a spider, a woman wearing flames, and a black race car.

Miss Trotter left her dolls to come over to them.

"Malcolm's started drawing again! Isn't it wonderful? He seems quite interested in drawing superheroes now. I wonder if he was a comic-book artist...." She gazed at the drawings a minute longer and then said, "Come give me your opinion over here."

Tish went off to find Wilma while Addie and Miss Trotter stood in front of her dolls and stuffed animals.

"I was planning on using the same Pilgrim and Native American clothes I made last year, but I had so much fun with my Cleopatra costume and making the Sphinx for Malcolm, I thought of an ancient Egyptian theme. I asked Minerva to look on her computer to see if the Egyptians had some fall festival....Would that be too strange?" She gave a little giggle. "You know, I think I'm just going to do it anyway. Who cares? It will give people something to talk about."

Ruby was parked outside Minerva's room with the foil helmet firmly in place in the front basket. Minerva's spear leaned beside the door, but Minerva herself was not at home.

There were, however, chirpy, chattery voices coming from the dining room.

Addie found Mrs. A, C, and D back at their favorite card table with, as their fourth, Minerva Swift.

"They finally talked me into it," said Minerva as Addie came over to them. "I decided I needed to get out more, and I must say, I'd forgotten how much mental energy is required in a good card game."

"She won't admit it," said Mrs. A, "but she's having fun."

"We're having a blast," said Mrs. D. "Minerva keeps us on our toes."

"And when it's not our turn," said Mrs. C, "we're still talking about the Halloween party, Addie, trying to figure out what really happened!"

Addie and Minerva had had long conversations about the Halloween party. They had seen Mr. Norris use his superpowers; they had both felt their memories melting away, had felt them come rushing back when his powers failed, and had witnessed the superheroes' arrival. But everyone else on Arborvine and at HVV seemed to have different ideas about what had really happened.

The headline story in the local paper that week helped confuse residents even more.

Gene Trippling had been the first to pick up a copy at the supermarket when he was getting groceries for himself and Patsy Firillo. He'd come back with as many copies as he could carry so everyone on Arborvine could have one.

SENIORS BRAWL AT HALLOWEEN PARTY! read the headline. The article began with: "It wasn't a happy Halloween last Saturday night at Happy Valley Village." The two reporters at the party had quotes from several residents, including many from Babs Duckworthy. Everyone had a different story. In the end, it was thought a string of lights must have shorted out and ignited a hay bale on fire, a power outage had caused an electrical malfunction, and though gusty winds hadn't been forecast, it was, after all, hurricane season and weird microburst storms had been known to happen before. There would be further reports when more information became available.

By the end of the story, which included a list of some of the crazier costumes and some of the residents' more bizarre explanations for what took place, the reporters' conclusion seemed to be that everyone at HVV was nuts.

Addie left the card players to their game. The lounge was quiet except for some opera wafting out of Mrs. Firillo's room and an argument between her and Mr. Trippling over the meaning of an Italian phrase.

Tish and Wilma huddled at the jigsaw puzzle table, going over Tish's application to the CNA program.

"Do you know if Mr. Norris is in his room?" Addie asked.

Wilma looked up.

"Unless he's flown out the window or something, I think our resident superhero is in there." She put down the booklet she was holding. "Now, Addie, I heard Mr. Norris and Des talking about some kind of surprise. Des won't tell me anything more. Do you know what it is?"

"No, but it's something to do with Des?"

"Addie told me she didn't know what it was," said Tish. "It's probably something Des is cooking up, like pizza or cupcakes, right?"

At Mr. Norris's door, Addie peeked in and saw him lying on his bed, fully clothed and sound asleep. She tiptoed in and sat in his comfy chair to wait for him to wake up and for the others to arrive.

She was wondering what her next map should be, maybe the old part of HVV with the tower, when a raspy throat-clearing came from the bed. Mr. Norris's eyes stayed shut.

"Did you see that blasted story in the paper?"

"Yeah, they made everyone here sound crazy. I thought you were asleep."

"Maybe it's better this way—a story about some old

farts won't be of much interest to the general public. Keep people from coming around."

There was silence, until a small snore woke Mr. Norris up again.

"One thing I still can't understand is how you got people to stand up to Obsidian's little army. Arborvine looked like they were ready to go to war." He opened one eye and stared at the ceiling. "I know it's boring around here, and they don't like the Sloat, and Patsy Firillo was upset at finding out Marcus Fox lied about being her nephew, and no one wants more land here turned into condos, but..."

"Did you ever think they did it for you?"

"Don't be ridiculous!" he growled. "If anything, they did it because YOU were asking them."

"Yeah, well, I'm thinking we're probably both right, though you won't admit it."

Two heads appeared around the edge of the door.

"Hi! Okay to come in?" said Marwa brightly. "Where's the surprise?" She looked around the room.

Dickson went straight to the window.

"Have you seen Marshall and Lucas hanging around? They keep wanting to come over and visit even though I keep telling them NO!" He pulled the curtains closed.

He saw Mr. Norris's black eyes trailing him.

"I know, Mr. Norris. I'll take care of it. I promise." Dickson sat in a heap on the floor. "It's not easy suddenly being the most popular guy at school. In fact, it's the WORST!"

"Well, do something about it before I move back to my house next week. I don't want eager little faces at my windows." Mr. Norris shuddered.

"Maybe you could have visiting hours one day a week," said Marwa. "You could do it here when you come for dinner every night like you said you would and not at your house. Ooo, we could sell tickets!"

"Marwa!!!" said everyone at once.

"Okay, okay, but maybe—"

There was a knock on the door and in came Des with his big smile.

"Hi, Mr. Norris....Are you ready?"

Mr. Norris cleared his throat and heaved himself up from his bed.

"Might as well get it over with. Though," he said eyeing the three kids, "don't expect too much. Des talked me into this little escapade. We'll see what happens."

"Where are we going?" said Marwa. "Where's the surprise?"

"Lead on, Des," said Mr. Norris. "And don't pester me, you three. You'll see."

They walked slowly over to the garage, where Des unlocked one of the big doors, opening both halves of it wide.

Mr. Norris took them over to look at his workshop.

"I can't wait to get back here." He looked at the drawings pinned above the workbench, and the bits and pieces of things left on the bench.

"What was I working on...ah, it was this old clock. But now I think I'll move on to this contraption." He tugged a cell phone from his pocket.

"You got one!" cried Dickson.

"Is this the surprise?" said Marwa.

"And what an annoyance!" said Mr. Norris. "I don't want to have to stick it in my pocket and I'm always losing it. I need to design a holder for it."

Marwa said, "I think they already have—" but stopped when Addie nudged her.

"Have you called THEM on it?" whispered Dickson.

"I suppose you mean the Guild? That's why I got the stupid thing. I felt I should at least call and thank them for what they did. We had a little meeting the other night."

It took a second for this fact to sink in.

"They came back here?" said Addie slowly.

"I made a deal with them," said Mr. Norris. "I handed in my badge and Guild card, and in return, the Guild's IT department, or whatever it's called, will erase the name Breathalyzer from the public record. I am officially retired and Breathalyzer no longer exists."

Marwa looked crushed.

Dickson too. He said, "You can DO that?" He thought a minute. "What about your suit?"

"Oh, I thought I'd give the suit to you little squirts, if you want it. And before you get too excited, remember it's faded, stretched out of shape, and does NOT have any special powers."

Marwa hopped up and down, clapping her hands.

"Ooo, is that the surprise?"

Meanwhile, Des had been quietly working in the main part of the garage.

He called to them.

"All set, Mr. Norris."

It was getting dark in the late afternoon, but the blue car, now that Des had taken off all the tarpaulins, shone and sparkled with a light all its own.

"Did I ever tell you I called it the Blue Zoom?" said Mr. Norris, going over to the car and running his fingers lightly along its side. "Des saw it the day you got rid of my father's papers and asked me about it."

Des walked around the car, touching it as carefully as he would a baby. "Mr. Norris asked me to take a look, and I did what I could, like changing the oil and spark plugs," he said. "And I drained the old gas out and managed to get E85 fuel, just like you said, Mr. Norris, but there are definitely parts in the engine I have never, ever seen before!"

"It is a beautiful car." Mr. Norris sighed.

"Mr. Norris, can I show them the engine?"

When Mr. Norris nodded, Des opened the hood.

"See those?" he said. "Those are the air intakes they call velocity stacks, and underneath there's a turbocharger and a supercharger. Man, you only see work like this in old F1 race cars." Des sighed happily. "And you wouldn't believe the crazy piping underneath. I don't know what's going on with that!"

"Des, you really fixed her up?" said Addie. She looked from him to Mr. Norris.

Dickson went and tugged at the cuff of Mr. Norris's jacket.

"Does she run?"

CHAPTER 35

L et's pull her out!" said Mr. Norris.

Addie stared at him. There was a gleam about him, and his dark eyes snapped with a sneaky sparkle. He looked like a kid who was up to something...and loving it.

He got in the driver's seat and released the brake. They managed, only with Des's help, to push the car out of the garage.

Des, his shoulder pressed hard against the hood, said, "Is this fiberglass? It's so light!"

"If you want to make a car fast," said Mr. Norris, patting the dashboard, "you add lightness."

When they had the car out on the gravel, everyone climbed in and took a look around, stroked the soft blue leather, and examined the dashboard with all its switches, screens, levers, knobs, and buttons.

There was a note sticking out of the glove compartment. It said *Check the trunk*.

Des went around and opened the trunk.

"Hey, what's this?"

Mr. Norris went to look.

"These canisters weren't here before," said Des.

Mr. Norris bent down for a closer look.

He snorted.

"Methanol! Must be a present from the Guild, a farewell gift! It makes the motor more powerful... at high altitude."

Mr. Norris and Des, whose eyes were full of questions, looked at each other.

Without any words, Addie could practically hear the conversation between them.

"Could we?" "Would it work?" "Should we?" "Want to?" "Why not?"

She had never seen Des or Mr. Norris smile so much.

While Mr. Norris showed Des how to transfer the methanol from the canisters to the car's special tank for it, Addie, Marwa, and Dickson hovered around them.

"Des," said Addie, "Wilma wanted to know if what we were doing was safe. Is this safe?"

Des grinned at Mr. Norris.

"Don't know!"

"We'll just turn her on and see what happens," said Mr. Norris with a chuckle. "One step at a time."

Des said, "Wait a second." He ran into the garage and came back wearing the leather racing car helmet and goggles he'd worn at the Halloween party. "I brought these just in case." He beamed.

None of them would ever forget that night. Mr. Norris sat in the driver's seat and turned the key. The others clustered around his open door. The motor roared and stuttered at first, but once it settled into the deep, raspy thrum of a motor tuned for full throttle, the next step was to go somewhere.

"It's dark. No one will see us," said Mr. Norris. "Where do you want to go?" He looked at them. "If you could go anywhere, where would it be?"

There was a burst of opinions from all sides that droned on and on until Addie managed to be heard.

"Home! I want to go home! To Mount Repose, Maine!"

Every pair of eyes fell on her.

"Maine! Are you crazy? That's way too far!" cried Dickson.

"Oh, no, it's not," said Mr. Norris softly. He looked at Addie. "Are you sure? Okay then, get in, everyone, let's try it. Let's go to Maine!"

"Wait, I need my map book!" Addie rushed upstairs to the apartment.

Once she was back, they all took their places: Mr. Norris in the driver's seat with Des beside him, the three kids in back. Addie had her map book open in front of her with a flashlight. She was explaining how to get there.

"First, I'll give you directions to Uncle Harry's. From there I have a map to get us to Uncle Tom's, and from there a map to Uncle Jim's, and then I know the way to Granny Lu's."

Des swung around from the front seat.

"Addie, what's the address? We can find it with GPS."

She looked at him.

"Oh." She gave him the address.

Des punched it into his phone.

Mr. Norris looked at the little screen.

"It shows which roads to take," said Des. "It'll make it real easy."

Mr. Norris looked at him.

"But we're not taking roads."

Mr. Norris flicked switches and worked the gearshift. The car backed up slowly, turned, and headed out the drive. The engine was loud enough to be a small plane. Addie hoped that was what the HVV residents would think it was.

When they got to the long, straight drive leading out of HVV, Mr. Norris began to work other controls and check the lighted dials. Des, beside him, watched every move he made. A high-pitched mechanical screech took over as the engine began to roar.

"Seat belts fastened?" yelled Mr. Norris over the noise.

The Blue Zoom began to charge down the driveway. Addie couldn't swallow, especially when Marwa threw her arms around her. Dickson, on Addie's other side, stared straight ahead, his eyes as big as they could get, his hands locked to the edge of the seat.

Even Des, as calm as they come, seemed to be having second thoughts as the car went faster and faster.

"Mr. Norris, I'm not sure we should—"

But he never finished the sentence.

A roar of engines kicked in from under their seat. The car shuddered and shook. Addie didn't know if she or the car would fall apart first.

Streetlights whipped past them, and then Addie, Dickson, and Marwa were slammed back against the blue leather seat as the nose of the Blue Zoom pulled up and took off. Into the air.

They started to breathe again as the car leveled off.

Dickson managed a whisper.

"NO...WAY!"

Addie and Marwa were too stunned to say anything, but Addie began to peel Marwa off her.

The big cities below were clusters of lights, but beyond them, once they got past Portland, Maine, the lights were few and far between.

It's funny how something so unbelievably magical can become kind of normal after a while.

"Can you turn up the heat?" said Dickson. "It's getting cold back here."

"What are we going to do when we get there?" said Marwa. "I mean, what can we see there? It's so dark!"

"That's a good question. Why, exactly, are we going to Mount Repose, Maine?" asked Mr. Norris, looking in the rearview mirror at them.

"There's something there that I need," said Addie.

"Something that got left behind. After Granny Lu died."

Marwa took Addie's hand in hers.

"I hope it doesn't make you sad," she said. "I think going back to Iraq would make me sad."

"I don't know if it will or not," said Addie, giving her hand a squeeze. "But it's something I really need."

Once they set down on the ground again, the GPS was much happier, recalibrated, and got them to Granny Lu's old house.

Addie stood looking at it, or as much of it as she could see in the dark. A baby stroller and some pots of dead flowers stood outside the door, so she guessed people were living there. But it looked smaller and sadder than she remembered. The rosebush was there and the lilac, but there was no gnome house underneath it. There was no birdbath or bird feeder. The flagpole was still there, and the little wishing well stood bravely over the well connection, but the dark, blank windows of the house and garage made it look dead and empty.

"Wow, it's dark around here!" said Des. "Are you sure people live here?"

"People go to bed early," said Addie. "But it helps for looking at the stars," she added, looking up.

"I'll say!" said Des, getting out of the car. The stars were strewn from one horizon to the other, a great bowl of glitter.

Marwa breathed deep.

"I love this!"

Mr. Norris pried himself out of the car with help from Des.

"Go get what you want, Addie," he said. "I think I'll wait here."

Addie got out Granny Lu's map.

"Does anyone have something I can use as a shovel?"

She followed her map to pace off six feet from the wishing well toward where she guessed the birdbath used to be while Dickson paced off thirteen feet from the house. Addie and Marwa started to dig with a screwdriver they'd found in the car. It took a few tries, but finally, about six inches down, they found the metal box.

After brushing dirt off it, Addie got back in the car and sat between Marwa and Mr. Norris in the backseat. Mr. Norris was letting Des's dream come true by letting him drive with Dickson as copilot.

While they sat in the driveway and Des checked the controls, Mr. Norris leaned forward.

"You can do it, Des. I'll be right here if you need me. Dickson, switch on that little lever over there so we can have some light back here."

Addie opened the metal box. It was a little bigger than a shoe box. Granny Lu had been about to throw it away once when she said, "This would be just about the right size for a Dream Box."

"What's that?"

"Oh, it's a box where you put all kinds of things you like to dream about. Here, take this postcard from Mrs. Leroux to start your collection."

That was the first postcard: the Golden Gate Bridge.

Inside the box, Addie found photos of herself, Granny Lu, and Tish. There were bits of tinsel, birthday cake candles, pictures cut from magazines of houses, of butterflies, of an owl. There were two bendy straws from a summer afternoon watching TV in the open garage. There were several of Granny Lu's famous commemorative coins ("Worth a million bucks one day!"), a lottery ticket, a fortune cookie, a brochure from one of Tish's ventures (Tish's Doggie Daycare and Spa).

"Are these things making you sad?" asked Marwa softly.

"No." Addie shook her head. "Well, not really. I'd forgotten some of them. Like, I don't know where these white stones came from. I remember this shell, though," she said, rubbing her fingers over the pearly inside. "And this was my favorite hair clip one of my best friends gave me. No, I'm really glad I have them again. They wouldn't mean anything to anyone else, but they mean something to me."

The box was still cold from being buried in the earth, but she had Marwa and Mr. Norris on either side of her to keep her warm.

Mr. Norris cleared his throat.

"Are you okay seeing your old house?"

"Yeah," she said softly. "But it sure isn't the same when the people aren't there anymore."

There were some papers in the bottom of the box. Addie unfolded them, brushing off sand and bits of tinsel.

"What are those?" asked Marwa.

"I used to make maps of big, fancy houses I was going to live in one day. I guess I put them in here because I didn't finish them. There's all this white space...."

"I don't know about you," Mr. Norris began, "but I kind of like white spaces. They're the parts that are 'Still to Be Explored.' Kind of like the Wild Wood on *The Wind in the Willows* map. They give you room to move, to explore. Maps can show where you've been, you know, but also where you might want to go someday."

Addie smiled.

"Granny Lu used to say that too."

A spotlight outside the house suddenly switched on, lighting up the whole front yard. The front door jerked open and a man was about to open the storm door, but seeing the gleaming blue car, he hesitated.

"Time to go home, Des!" called Mr. Norris from the backseat.

The man never took his eyes off them and continued to stare long after they were just another blip in the starry sky. One with red taillights.

End

ACKNOWLEDGMENTS

With every book I've had published at Holiday House, Mary Cash has been there to edit, encourage, and guide my manuscript through to a printed book. I am in awe of the amount of time and work she and the others at Holiday House put into the effort. The whole team is amazing: Kerry Martin, Raina Putter, Barbara Perris, Terry Borzumato-Greenberg, Michelle Montague, Sara DiSalvo, and many whom I will never meet. Thank you to all of them.

Since my expertise in many areas is limited, I've relied on friends and family. I'm grateful to Ronnie Wilson and Lea McCrone for help with nursing questions. Thank you, Erin, for the photo!

My two wonderful sons are always ready to help with their mother's crazy questions. Ned Swain dreamed up what a superhero's car might look and sound like. Bob Swain came up with ideas for a superhero's superpowers and the spiffy title. My heartfelt thanks to them both.